CONSEQUENCES

By Shirley Guendling

*To Nancy,
All the best!
Hugs,
Shirley
xo xo*

Consequences

All Rights Reserved

COPYRIGHT © 2022 Shirley Guendling

This book may not be reproduced, transmitted, or stored in whole or in part by any means, including graphic, electronic, or mechanical, without the express written consent of the publisher except in the case of brief questions embodied in critical articles and reviews.

ISBN: ISBN: 978-1-7371538-3-2

Cover design by Sooraj Mathew

Edited by Hilary Jastram, Bookmark Publishing House

https://jhillmark.com/

Dedication

I dedicate this book to my late husband, Don. His encouragement and support were always there for just about any word I wrote. "Oh boy, that sounds great. Keep that chapter going." "You're doing such a good job." Those were the comments I would hear from him all the time. I would smile, knowing all the cheering on, true or not true, came from love.

And ... for Hilary Jastram, who started out as my editor and became my "adopted granddaughter" and very dear and treasured friend. There would be no book if not for Hilary and her fabulous input and coaching!

Get in Touch with Shirley!

https://www.facebook.com/shirley.guendling

Contents

Dedication
Prologue
Chapter 1 1
Chapter 2 7
Chapter 3 13
Chapter 4 21
Chapter 5 25
Chapter 6 31
Chapter 7 37
Chapter 8 45
Chapter 9 53
Chapter 10 63
Chapter 11.. 69
Chapter 12 81
Chapter 13 87
Chapter 14 95
Chapter 15 103
Chapter 16 111
Chapter 17 119
Chapter 18 129
Chapter 19 137
Chapter 20 143
Chapter 21 155
Acknowledgments
About the Author

Prologue

Mid-December

Claire Kendall was deep in sleep in her king-size bed, snuggled under her down comforter, when she rolled over and found herself in the midst of a full-fledged panic attack.

What happened?

Did I have a bad dream?

Was I dreaming of my past or the premonition of a horrible future?

Whatever it was, she was terrified. There was so much turmoil going on in her head. A memory, just out of reach. Her whole body vibrated with tension as she broke into a cold sweat.

Suddenly, overcome with nausea, she shoved the comforter back and rushed to the bathroom. There, she collapsed to her knees, hugging the toilet bowl.

All she could do was vomit over and over again until she felt turned inside out. Her illness was so violent that she soiled her pink satin nightgown, and dammit! She'd missed the bowl a couple of times, too. She cried a little, knowing she couldn't just crawl back to her bed, totally confused and scared.

She leaned into the bowl for round two, then finally, the vomiting stopped. Even though she felt like a rag, she got to her feet and stood there trembling. She had to clean everything up—at least a good rinse.

After that, she slid into bed, thinking the worst was over. But she couldn't have been further from the truth. It wasn't just her guts that were turning inside out. It was her life.

How It All Started

Chapter 1

The Previous November

As Claire stepped into her company's holiday party, it was obvious that all the partygoers had been there for quite a while. Everyone was all revved up, and lots of noise filled the room.

What else would you expect from a global marketing company? Our job makes us expert partiers—even on a Wednesday, she figured grimly. *Gross.*

She'd driven the short distance from her posh penthouse to the corporate office on Michigan Avenue and refused the valet parking. A large bar was set up at the back, and people lingered with drinks in their hands or milled about waiting to place their order. The hum of chatter and the clash of too much aftershave and perfume—a pet peeve of Claire's—was nauseating. Claire always wore the same fragrance. Heavy scents were not for her. Her signature scent was a light, clean aroma with a touch of floral.

Then she zeroed in on an open spot at the bar and jostled her way to the front. When she finally got the bartender's attention, she ordered a glass of Cabernet—her third of the night. Just twenty minutes before, Claire had gotten the party started before she'd even set foot out her front door. Thoughts of better times with Alan, the promise of their life together had all swirled in her head like the Cabernet in her glass that she sipped overlooking the slice of Lake Michigan. That was her happy place. Even through the thick pane of glass she could smell the fresh water and sense the misty wind on her face. The view from her high-rise transported her.

Claire came back to Earth as she waited for her wine and turned to survey the room. She would be back to her happy place soon enough. The men were all dressed in suits and ties—with one exception. Scotty, the new hire, was wearing a kiwi-green golf shirt.

Apparently, no one had advised the poor kid that his choice of attire would not fit the bill. Claire felt sorry for Scotty, but he wasn't her worry, so she quickly put him out of her mind. There wasn't a man in the room that interested her. They were all paunchy, from the alcohol, no doubt. The women didn't fare much better. Most of them had that well-worn look that screamed, "I have been here too long."

In contrast to their tired faces, the women had tried to perk themselves up with black-tie dresses and satin and sparkly shoes. Of course, like any office party, everyone was smiling and pretending to be best buddies. *Maybe they're in line for a big bonus or raise,* Claire thought. *I guess they need to look their best when they smile and accept it.*

Several small tables were set up around the room. As Claire stepped between them, she searched for Eleanor—Ellie—and Vida, her coworkers, who she spotted sitting in the far corner. A few months earlier, she would have floated into the party with Alan on her arm. He would have held open the gleaming glass doors and smiled as he pulled out her chair, maybe brushed a kiss on the top of her hand. As she made her way to a long appetizer table, so laden with every kind of finger food it was a wonder it didn't collapse, she smiled uneasily at the people around her. It was just her now. She would never get used to going anywhere alone again. For the thousandth time, since a drunk driver had killed Alan, she ordered herself to toughen up and swallowed back the lump in her throat.

Blinking forcefully a few times to chase away her tears, Claire grabbed a small plate and selected a few of her favorite foods to nibble on before joining Ellie and Vida. As she neared their table, she held up her wine glass and smiled. "Claire," Ellie said with a bright grin. "Pull up a chair."

Vida raked her eyes over Claire's figure and exclaimed, "Wow, you look sensational in that dress. All your best curves show to perfection. Way to go!" Claire smiled and murmured a small "Thank you." Vida patted the chair beside her, and Claire sat down.

The conversation flowed smoothly. The three women considered each other friends. They mostly talked about how no one knew who was up for a promotion, bonus, or whatever—although everyone really did know, as is the case with all office gossip. As Claire munched on her appetizers, she enjoyed herself more than she thought she would. Since Alan had died, right before their wedding, she was surprised that she could smile or laugh at all.

In the next moment, she felt as though someone was watching her, and the skin on her arms erupted in goosebumps. She scanned the room until she caught the eye of Bryce Hollingsworth, the CEO of the agency. *Whoa, Claire thought, maybe I'm getting a raise, a bonus, or even a promotion. I wonder if he'll present it to me?* For all the years that Bryce had been CEO of the firm, Claire hadn't thought much of him, although she knew all the other women in the office were ga-ga over his piercing blue eyes. He didn't say more than two words to her most days, so his intense stare threw her.

When she looked directly at him, he stared right through her. It was nothing like Alan setting his eyes upon her. Alan's had also been blue, but they'd been warm and usually surrounded by crinkles at the edges because he'd smiled so much.

Bryce wasn't tall as Alan had been, but he was powerfully built and broad. His graying hair at the temples only gave him more of a distinguished air. His ever-present monogrammed handkerchiefs and tailor-made suits made him a bit of a snob—and a turnoff. His presence and the proof he knew she was alive did nothing for her. It was another sign that no one compared to Alan.

Claire smiled at Bryce and turned back to her friends, still feeling his eyes boring into her head. She tried to forget the sensation as she focused on relaxing with Vida and Ellie.

As a good friend always does, Ellie said, "Claire, honey, you have spinach in your teeth. Doesn't make for the sexiest smile, girlfriend." Claire thanked Ellie with her hand over her mouth as she dug out her compact to check out the damage. "Oh lovely," she said, slipping the compact back into her purse and rising from the table. "Save my chair, and I'll take care of my green teeth."

As she walked to the ladies' room opposite the huge room, Claire passed groups of people having drinks and fun. She smiled at the ones she knew.

She entered the hallway to the powder room and immediately heard footsteps behind her on the marble floor. *Maybe someone else has spinach in their teeth, too.* She smiled with her lips closed at her inside joke.

Her heart pounded a little, but she chastised herself for being silly. The ladies' room was just ahead, and she hastened to reach it.

Then someone grabbed her arm and shoved her into the men's room. Once inside, the person turned her around to face him. Bryce Hollingsworth glowered as he locked the door. He leveled her with a sick sneer and said, "I've been eyeing you for the longest time. Don't tell me you weren't flirting with me." Claire shook her head, unable to speak. "Just remember this is what you wanted to happen," he whispered in a gravelly voice. Claire shoved him off her and yelled, "What the hell is the matter with you?" Bryce's eyes hardened as he grabbed his monogrammed handkerchief out of his pocket and shoved it into Claire's mouth. He slammed her up against the wall, grabbing her wrists in one hand. Claire's mouth dropped as he unzipped his fly, and his fingers searched around her scanty bikini panties until he found what he was looking for, then he shoved himself inside her. She squirmed and fought against him, tears streaming down her face as he slammed her into the tile wall, but he was a lot stronger, and she couldn't get away. All she could do was try not to choke on his handkerchief that tasted of chemicals and reeked of his woodsy cologne.

When he was satisfied, Bryce relaxed his grip on her just long enough for her to ram her body full force into his.

Bryce's eye grew wide as he teetered on his heels, and he fell backward, hitting the tile floor with a hideous thud. Then he went still. Claire yanked his handkerchief out of her mouth, gagging as she crumpled it up and jammed it in her bag. She stared at him, panting, her heart thudding out of control, waiting to see a flutter of movement. But he didn't stir. He just lay there with his eyes open, staring at the ceiling. Claire felt the room shrink around her. *Oh, my God,* she thought, *nooooo, he can't be dead! Oh no, please, God!* She had to get out of there. *Someone's going to see me!*

She pulled herself together, splashed water on her face, dried herself off, smoothed her hair, rearranged her clothing, then picked up her evening bag and made for the door, wishing her high heels didn't clack so loudly. After checking the hallway to be sure no one was there, she walked out of the men's room.

Claire wasn't sure if she could act nonchalantly and as if everything was as normal as it was before. She hoped no one would notice her shaking legs or hair that still looked a little out of place. Everything was out of place now.

When she got back to her table, Vida locked eyes on hers. "What took you so long? We were just about to send a search party. Oh, you look pale. Are you sick?"

"I think some of the appetizers didn't sit too well in my stomach." Claire could barely get the words out. Her stomach genuinely was upset now, and panic made her teeth chatter.

"Maybe you better go home," murmured Ellie. "Do you want me to drive you?"

"I can get home on my own, thanks." Claire offered a tiny smile. "I sure turned out to be a party pooper," she said with a grimace.

"Don't even think about it. Just go get some rest. Maybe some Pepto Bismol, or whatever. Feel better!" ordered Vida.

"Okay, see you tomorrow. Hope the rest of the party goes great, and each of you wins big bonuses—but steer clear of the food," Claire joked, hoping she sounded sincere.

I have to get out of here.

The party was in full swing as Claire crept slowly out of the room. Everyone around her seemed to laugh too loud. She painted a grim smile on her face and sidestepped people clustered everywhere. Thankfully no one stopped her to make small talk or ask where she was going. She made it to the elevator, downstairs, and to her car, all while trying to keep herself from falling apart. After fastening herself into her seatbelt, her tears finally fell. *I just have to make it a few blocks*, she told herself. *Why is the drive home so much longer?*

When Claire finally made it home, she dug her key out of her purse, her hands shaking so hard she nearly couldn't get it in the lock. She opened the door, darted inside, then turned and locked it. Finally safe, she collapsed right there on the front mat, sobbing and screaming. Even when it seemed like she was done, she would start all over again.

After some time, she crawled over to the couch and climbed onto the cushions. Her body hurt where Bryce had brutalized her, and she was shaking and still in shock as she lay there in the fetal position. "Damn you, Hollingsworth. Damn you to hell! Which is probably where you are!" she yelled between hysterical sobs. Softer, she cried, "Alan, where are you? I can't do this without you …"

Chapter 2

It was so late it was nearly morning when Claire finally undid herself from her rigid position on the couch. She stood up and pulled herself out of her dress and shoes. As she yanked off the dress so fiercely she nearly ripped it off her body; she swore she would never wear it again. With the same ferocity, she got rid of the rest of her clothes, the hose, her blood-streaked underwear, and bra, balling them up and burying them in the bottom of the trash can.

She jammed her evening bag into the back bottom drawer of her dresser. "I don't need another reminder," she choked out as she slammed the drawer shut. Then she finally made it to the shower, trembling and dizzy as the water blasted her.

She tried as hard as possible to scrub away the night, turning the water up to the highest temperature she could tolerate. Steaming water poured over her wrecked body.

After her shower, she headed straight for her bed, unsure if she would be able to sleep. Pulling the covers tight around her at least made her feel a little more secure.

As her mind and heart slowed, she drifted off. Then the phone rang, jolting her awake and sending her into another panic.

She answered the phone through a constricted throat. "Hello?"

Ellie screamed, "You won't believe what happened after you left. Oh my God, this is so terrible!"

"What are you talking about?" Claire dreaded hearing Ellie's answer. A stone dropped in her stomach.

"Bryce Hollingsworth is dead! DEAD, Claire."

"DEAD!? What happened?" Claire asked, holding her breath as Ellie rushed on. "They found him in the men's room. He must've fallen and hit his head. There wasn't any blood or anything. I guess the injury was all inside his skull. You won't believe all the goings-on after he was discovered."

Claire listened, but she didn't hear anything as Ellie rattled on. She forced herself to sit up on the side of the bed and hold her screams in until she had hung up the phone. Her legs jittered in her fresh, clean nightgown.

"Scotty found his body. This is just unbelievable. Claire, thank heavens you went home. I wish I would've driven you!"

Claire snapped to a little and uttered, "No, Ellie—"

But Ellie was off and running again, "Oh, and his fly was open like he was about to go to the urinal." Ellie started crying. "This is so unreal!"

Claire slowed her breathing as Ellie plowed on with all the details. She knew she would have to be very careful with her responses and not sound over the top—shocked, or hysterical. *Shut up, Ellie*, her mind kept repeating on a loop. *How am I supposed to listen to this?*

Claire cleared her throat and said as normally as she could muster, "Ellie, this is unbelievable. How is everyone else in the office handling it?"

So here was the awful truth. As much as Claire had tried to convince herself otherwise, Bryce was dead, and she was his killer. *Dear God, how could this have happened?* The nightmare she would never be rid of floated around in her head. She had murdered her boss. Would anyone suspect her?

Ellie exhaled loudly into the phone. "Vida is as shook up as I am, but she is doing a better job of keeping her cool. I'm totally freaked out," moaned Ellie.

If only I hadn't eaten that spinach appetizer. If only the spinach hadn't stuck in my teeth. If only Ellie hadn't told me about it.

Their conversation ended with each of them promising to call each other if they had any more news.

About an hour later, Ellie called Claire again. "I'm sorry, but we are not going to sleep tonight. I just heard they are transporting Bryce to the East Coast, where his family lives, so there won't be a service unless they do a memorial ... Do you think they'll have one?"

"Ellie, I don't—"

Ellie butted in, "It will obviously all be private. Oh, and one other thing, the office will be closed for the next two days, out of respect and, I am sure, to figure out who will replace Bryce."

"Thanks, Ellie," Claire murmured, knowing she spoke like a robot but hoping she could pass off her tone as exhaustion. "That all makes sense ... if any sense can be made of this. But, El, I really gotta sleep now."

"I'll quit calling, sorry. Yes, get some rest," Ellie said softly.

Claire hung up the phone, but she didn't lie down again. She paced and wrung her hands. *What the hell should I do next?*

As the sun peeked through her windows, Claire scolded herself to get to bed and at least pretend to sleep.

When she woke up, it was three hours later.

Somehow, Claire got through the day.

She tried to eat but didn't have much luck.

Watching TV was useless, too, as her mind constantly raced back to the scene in the men's room—the scene she would relive for the rest of her life. There was no escape from her new reality. No Alan to wrap her up in his arms and soothe her. She was on her own, and she was a killer.

☙

The next morning, Claire felt she couldn't tolerate the stress of trying to cope with what had happened alone. She was going to explode! *Should I call Chloe? She's the big sister. She's the real adult. I know she'll fix all of this! But wait, is it a better idea to call Ellie? I can't hold this inside …*

Either prospect felt like a risk.

In the end, Claire phoned Ellie and asked her to come over right away. "I think I might be in trouble. Please, I can't tell you about it over the phone."

Ellie's first words when she arrived at Claire's apartment were, "Claire, what's the matter?" You sounded so awful on the phone, not like yourself at all! And you look TERRIBLE!" Ellie said. It was true.

Claire hadn't combed her hair; she wore no makeup, and her eyes were red and swollen. "What's going on?" Ellie asked.

"I don't know how to tell you this," Claire said. "And I hate to burden you with it, but I have to tell somebody!" Claire started sobbing uncontrollably. Ellie let her cry for a few minutes until she composed herself. Claire grasped Ellie's hands and implored, "Obviously, before I begin, you have to understand this is all strictly confidential." Ellie's eyes grew big. "Of course, Claire, I would never violate your confidence."

After Claire told Ellie the entire surreal story, she was relieved and exhausted.

Ellie was shocked, sickened, and furious. "Claire, this is so unbelievable. I'm having trouble trying to absorb this. You poor thing! I am heartbroken for you. That monster, Bryce, maybe he got what he deserved!"

"No, Ellie, he shouldn't have had to DIE!" Claire brought her voice down to a normal level. "But now I have to cope with this and try to live as if it never happened. How can I ever forgive myself?"

"Claire, I'm sorry, but I have to ask, why didn't you run out of the men's room and tell us what had happened? That way, you wouldn't be carrying around this guilt, as if any of this was your fault anyway," said Ellie.

"I thought about that, of course. Turned it over and over in my mind. I didn't think anyone would believe me. The only other answer I can give is that for some reason I felt ashamed—as if it was my fault. I didn't want people to know. I felt not only violated but also dirty. Does that make any sense at all?" Claire said.

"Yes, but oh, Claire, if you had only reported it right after it happened. No one would blame you. I'm not saying they will now. It's just ... more complicated." Both women realized that no matter how much they overthought about it, there was no easy answer as to where they were supposed to go from there.

"How about a cup of tea? Or something stronger? Can we just sit and relax together?" asked Ellie.

"Thanks, Ellie, but no matter how long we sit and TRY to relax, the shitty truth is, nothing will change! I have to return to work and try my best to act as if nothing happened. How I will manage that, I have no idea. Just the thought of going back into that building makes my heart race!" Claire tugged at the sleeve of her cashmere sweater, fighting off a chill.

Ellie's eyes softened as she looked at Claire. She could see the love in Ellie's eyes. "How about we arrange to meet where we park our cars and go into the building together—or do you think people would notice it's something new and question it?" Ellie said.

"That's so sweet of you, Ellie. Thank you, but no, if I am going to do this, and I am, I have to do it on my own. I suppose everyone will still be buzzing like crazy about Bryce."

"Yeah, probably, but try to look calm. I know you can do it, Claire!"

"I most certainly will. Monday, I will be miss wide-eyed and act so interested! How does that sound?"

"Great! I'll do the same. I'm with you in this, and you can lean on me anytime," Ellie said with a sincere smile. Her demeanor was always happy. She was the perfect bouncy California girl with her long, straight blonde hair, engaging blue eyes, and slim physique. In that moment, she was more beautiful on the inside—but then again, Ellie always was. Claire would have described her as a godsend.

Chapter 3

When Monday finally arrived, Claire and Ellie walked into the office separately, but Claire knew Ellie was with her in spirit. She could reach out to her no matter what. Ellie was her ride or die! They both did their best to act interested in the chatter about Bryce's death but were cautious not to give away what they knew.

Still, all day long, Claire barely held it together as people gossiped excitedly about Scotty finding his body, his closed head wound, and how he had died with his fly wide open. A few times, Claire excused herself and rushed to the bathroom. She exploded through the door and steadied herself against the sink.

"Just a few more hours," she whispered to herself as she wet paper towels, then pressed them to her face, her hands shaking. When she closed her eyes, all she could see was Bryce's face looming at hers. His mouth twisted up, his eyes unyielding as he pressed her against the wall. Tears welled up in her eyes and threatened to roll down her cheeks. She shook her head vigorously and ordered herself, "Stop crying right this second. You are going to go out there and do your job. If someone wants to talk about him, you will tell them you have work to do." Then with a firm squaring of her shoulders, she yanked open the door and headed back to her desk. As she walked toward her cube, she heard more hushed voices. "But what do you think will happen to our jobs?" "Who do you think will take over?" "I hope it's not that asshole marketing director …" Claire swallowed hard and rushed past everyone hanging around each other's workstations. She slipped into her chair and plugged her headphones into her ears.

Throughout the day, Ellie gave Claire warm, empathetic smiles. Claire gave her small smiles back. She couldn't do better than that, not when her heart was leaping in her chest, she was sweating through her dress, and she had to keep hiding her trembling hands. At least the drama of Bryce's death took the spotlight off her and allowed her to mostly process what had happened without any extra attention.

It was bad enough that it happened at all, she thought, as she tried for the millionth time to read a client's copy.

Vida drifted over just then, and Claire snapped back to the present. She blearily registered that Vida had a new haircut and had poured herself into a beautiful new periwinkle outfit. She mustered up some interest in her friend.

"Vida, you look sensational! New do and new duds, just great," Claire smiled.

Vida gave her usual half-grin and said, "Thanks! I took advantage of the two days off—just needed Bryce to die to get them, I guess."

Claire did her best to chuckle as Vida's words slugged her in the gut.

After more dragged-out hours and two more trips to the ladies' room to compose herself, Claire finally grabbed her jacket off the back of her chair and slipped out of the building without anyone seeing her. As she sat in her car, hunched low in the driver's seat, Claire sobbed in her hands. She let everything spill out once more and hoped it would be the last time she would cry about her assault but doubted it. After a few minutes, she mopped her makeup mess off her face, put her car in gear, and steered toward home.

In the lobby of her apartment complex, Claire stopped to pick up her mail, then took the elevator to her floor. She flipped through the envelopes, at first seeing the usual notices, the electric bill, a reminder from her dentist to make an appointment and so on.

Then her fingers hit on a plain white envelope with no return address. *That's odd*, she thought as she stepped into her apartment and tore open the envelope.

Inside was a loose sheet of paper with a message in large type: "DID YOU LOSE SOMETHING?"

Chills swept over Claire's body, but she didn't know why. *What on earth could this mean?* she thought as she stared at the letter. After coming up blank on any reason she would've received it, she tossed it onto her kitchen counter. "It's a mistake," she said, slumping her way to the couch. "But I can't take anything else happening today. Not one thing." Tears pricked her eyes, and she swallowed around the lump in her throat as she stepped out of her shoes and curled into a ball on the couch. There, finally, in the safety of her home, she let the tears fall as long as they needed to.

∽

As the days passed, the office drama died down, and everyone went back to being their normal workmate selves. Scotty didn't appear to be missing Bryce at all. As he peacocked around the office, each day growing more obnoxious, he acted as though he'd been named the new company "welcome committee of one." He appeared to have no self-awareness as he greeted everyone each morning with an overzealous handshake and smile. At first, people got a kick out of his new act, but as he repeated his gesture, Claire could see most were getting uncomfortable. They'd utter a nervous laugh and back away from him as they practically speed-walked to their desks.

Claire knew how they felt. When Scotty pumped her hand, he held it a little too long until she ripped it from him and muttered under her breath, "Knock it off, Scotty."

Vida wasn't nearly as restrained. "What brought this on?" she strode over to the two of them to scold him and laser a warning glare with her amber eyes. "Cut it out, mister. You're making everyone squirm. Not cute!" She grabbed Claire's wrist and turned on her heel, taking Claire away with her.

Somehow, Claire made it through another day. She figured out that if she avoided the side of the building where Bryce's office had been, she could keep a measure of control. Still, she felt a little sick to her stomach every day and only managed to eat a bite or two of her lunch.

But Claire was a fighter, and after some time, she was angrier than anything else. Anger saved her life. It forced her to get back to her old routines. On mild winter days, when she didn't feel like driving, she started window shopping on her way home from work again. She shopped a little online and bought herself trinkets and treats. She Netflixed shows to escape what she couldn't wrap her mind around yet. Most importantly, she began to think of Alan once more.

She had wanted to keep the memories of him and slimeball Bryce from ever meeting in her thoughts, so she had frozen Alan out. What they'd had was too precious to let Bryce taint it. But now, as she healed, and realized that life was one big tangle of emotions, she cut herself a break.

As she went through her emotions, suddenly she was sad that it had happened at all. That Bryce was a permanent part of the fabric of her life. The one good bit she could take from it was that it was in the past. He couldn't hurt her anymore. She was in charge of how badly she let him affect her. Knowing this, she fought as hard as possible every day to stay positive, to look forward to the rest of her life—whatever that would be. *Lonely*, she figured. On top of losing Alan and feeling that she would be alone, the rape had sent her into a protective recess in her mind where she couldn't even imagine ever letting a man in.

As Claire settled into the new reality of her life, for the most part, life went on—until one day, it ground to a halt again.

She was on her way into the elevator; her mail clutched in her hand, when she spied another anonymous plain envelope. Inside was a similar note written on the same kind of paper as the last one. This note screamed: "AREN'T YOU MISSING SOMETHING?"

Now Claire was spooked. Her knees grew weak. *The first note was not an accident.*

"Who the hell is sending these notes and why?" she said as she slammed the envelope on the kitchen counter.

The worst thing about the notes was the time in between receiving them. It was then that Claire let her guard down. She still struggled to eat much of the time but thought that had to do with her ongoing stress, denial, struggle—you name it. The nightmares continued, and she would sit straight up in bed from a dead sleep, a scream still on her lips. *Why can't I shake Bryce from my mind?*

Sometimes, she would scream into her pillowcase from the sheer frustration of being unable to reclaim her life fully. That's when the nausea was the worst. She didn't grow weaker from it. Instead, she got mad again. Her emotions had her dancing like a puppet. *Why is this happening to me and after losing Alan? Should I have gone right to the police? At least told someone at the party?* Knowing the consequences of her actions had created part of her challenges, she wasn't just angry at Bryce but at herself. *I couldn't have pushed him off?* In those moments she wrestled with the most fury even though she knew she couldn't have done anything to save herself from him. Bryce had been twice as big, and it was logical, but she couldn't believe it.

When she received the third white envelope, Claire nearly passed out. She crumpled the letter in her fist, the words on the note emblazoned in her mind: "THIS ITEM IS YOURS! I KNOW IT IS!"

Claire tossed the note in the direction of the kitchen counter and collapsed onto her couch, writhing with her head in her hands. *What could it be? What item am I missing, and why does it even matter?* Of course, her mind went immediately back to the night with Bryce. The worst moment of her life, besides losing Alan. *Am I in trouble? I am a murderer.*

She could feel the blood drain from her face as she dashed to her bedroom and yanked out the bottom dresser drawer. She hadn't brought much to the office party, just herself and her bag. She pawed through her clothes, grabbed her bag, and spilled the contents onto the carpet. Just the sight of the symbols of that night struck fear in her. Tears leaked from her eyes as she studied the items at her feet. It didn't come to her right away. But then she noticed something was missing. An item she was never without since it had been given to her so long ago. *No compact!* It was one of her most treasured possessions, that and the watch with the diamond-chipped numerals Alan had given her for their six-month anniversary. Claire remembered the day her parents had given her the compact. It was her twenty-first birthday and Claire was so taken with the feeling of the cool gold trinket with the engraved initial "C" sitting in her hand. "Just tuck this away, sweetie, and you can think of your father and I every time you touch up your beautiful face," her mom had said in her sweet voice. She and her dad had been gone for seven years now. She still missed them every day.

Claire felt her eyes grow wide as various scenarios ran through her mind. Dropping it on the floor in the bathroom, outside of the bathroom, near his body. It couldn't be anything else, or why would whoever had sent the notes make such a big deal?

Someone had picked it up and kept it, but who?

Claire crumpled to the carpet and started crying again. *This is all I do now*, she thought, crazed with the unknown.

Nausea overtook her suddenly, and she groaned. *I can't let what Bryce did kill me*, she thought. *I'm going to force myself to eat all my dinner tonight.* That was it. Claire crammed everything on the carpet back in her purse and stuffed it in the drawer again.

Then a different wave hit her. The wave of realization. *On no! I missed my period!*

She stormed out of the bedroom and into the living room, pulling at her hair. "That will NOT be the reason! Please, God, I am begging you ... Do NOT let me be pregnant!"

Claire remembered the day she had stopped taking birth control. It was one day after Alan had died. One day of being awash in memories and knowing she had to hold on extra tight to them because there would be no more. That realization sent her into a fresh crying fit. She simply could not comprehend losing him. She hadn't been able to comprehend it when she was charged with writing his eulogy and not when his casket was lowered into the ground. Moments they had shared collided into her as she cried about the baby she might be carrying, the baby she had planned to share with Alan. Her first of what they had planned to be at least two.

When they were engaged, she had thought about how it would feel to tell him she was about to make him a daddy. She had dreamt about it.

"It's not supposed to happen this way!" Claire hollered at the ceiling then wondered fleetingly what her neighbors thought of all her yelling and screaming of late.

She grabbed her car keys in a panic and drove to the nearest pharmacy to purchase a handful of pregnancy tests. As she sped down the road, her heart in her throat, she kept repeating softly, "Please let this test be negative. It just HAS TO BE negative."

Claire stormed through the pharmacy doors, got her tests, and headed home. She tried to stay focused on her driving, but it was nearly impossible.

Once inside her apartment, she couldn't get the wrapping off the package fast enough. She immediately took the test, uttering a silent prayer as she did. Her heart galloped in her chest. *I just want the whole thing to go away!*

When the alarm on her cell phone went off, she forced herself to walk slowly to the counter where three of the tests were. All of them were positive. Claire felt the air go out of her lungs and slumped against the sink. Her head swam with the truth. She was afraid she would faint and hit her head on the floor like …

"No, no, no!" Claire found the strength to stand. She scooped up the tests in her hands and hurled them at the mirror.

Then she called Ellie and, without telling her what was going on, begged her to come over *right now*. Within fifteen minutes Ellie was there. She was one of those friends who just knew when she was needed. Ellie was the caretaker in their group of three. The second she was in Claire's door, Ellie pulled her into a hug. The two women embraced, and Ellie stepped back, her hands lingering on Claire's arms. "What's wrong?" she said, her concerned eyes glued to Claire's.

"You better sit down for this one," Claire smiled weakly and gestured at the sofa.

Chapter 4

"So after everything that happened and Alan dying and then I stopped taking the pill and—"

Ellie's mouth formed a perfect "O" as her eyes flew wide in shock. "Oh, Claire, no! This cannot be happening."

Claire was totally numb. She sat there next to her best friend, incapable of accepting any words coming out of her mouth. "I wasn't planning on having sex with anyone—obviously. If only I hadn't stopped taking it. Now I have a whole new nightmare—Bryce Hollingsworth's baby!"

"What are you going to do?"

"I don't know." Claire wrung her hands. "I haven't thought about anything beyond finding out literally twenty minutes ago that I am pregnant."

"Oh, sweetie, I am so, so sorry," Ellie soothed, resting her hand on Claire's.

"Me, too," Claire said through her tears. All she could picture was a giant drain, and her dreams getting sucked right down it. *Who am I anymore?* She wouldn't be able to answer that question for a long time.

Ellie stayed with Claire for several hours, and they discussed all the different scenarios for Claire keeping and not keeping the baby. Nothing was decided. They just kept circling the subject; her emotions were too new.

Suddenly, Claire burst out, "I haven't even told you about the notes!"

"What are you talking about?"

So Claire explained as Ellie leaned in to listen.

"What in the world is going on, Claire? Do you have any idea who would send them?"

Claire shrugged. "Not a clue. It's very unnerving."

Ellie suggested she could stay longer and offered to buy them dinner. Claire tried to refuse, but Ellie was insistent. "You have to eat, sweetie, now, more than ever. You have to take care of yourself—and the baby—even if it's a short-term resident."

Ellie didn't wait for Claire's response but picked up her phone and ordered Chinese food. The thought of it made Claire's stomach roil again.

As Ellie busied herself in Claire's kitchen, clattering dishes and silverware, Claire walked over to the huge windows and took in the gorgeous Chicago skyline. Just like that, her life was out of control. She tried to mentally assimilate everything that had happened so quickly. An impending storm was going to make everything worse. A dark cloud had infiltrated her very soul.

When the food arrived, they settled on the couch, their meal spread out on the coffee table. Ellie plucked a fortune cookie up from the mix of soy and duck sauce packets and chopsticks. "Should we wait to open our fortune cookies until after dinner, or do it now? I'm always so curious."

Claire smiled robotically at Ellie. "Either way is okay with me," she sighed. "I think most of my bad fortune has already been decided."

"I'll go first then," Ellie said brightly, and Claire could tell she was trying to cheer her up. "Here's goes nothing," Ellie said as she cracked open her cookie with a snap. "You have big travel plans ahead," Ellie read. "Well, I don't have any travel plans that I know of." She raised her eyebrows. "But it sounds great. Now you." She handed Claire a cookie.

Cautiously Claire broke open her cookie. "There will be someone new in your future." Claire shrieked and threw the cookie into the delivery bag. "As if I didn't know that already!" Claire sat back on the couch and crossed her arms, refusing to meet Ellie's eyes. "You'll have to excuse me, looks like

I'll be crying again. My new favorite pastime."

"You can cry in front of me any day. I hope you know that," Ellie said gently. Claire's tearstained eyes caught Ellie's soft ones. "I know," she whispered. "I just need some time to figure out what to do. I'm sorry. I'm a terrible host."

"Silly," Ellie chastised and took Claire's hands. "You'd have to do more than that to offend me. You know, like insult my mom, or tell me my hair is awful," Ellie smiled.

Claire laughed in spite of everything then grew quiet. "Thank you. I'm all cried out and exhausted."

After they'd eaten, Ellie said, "Let me get out of your hair then, and you get some rest," She gathered up the empty cartons and brought them to the kitchen. She stopped at the doorway and turned back to Claire. "Will you be okay?"

"I just need to rest, but don't worry about me."

"As if that's possible."

Claire thanked Ellie profusely for the dinner, the ear, and being a friend she could always count on, then managed to see her to the door.

After Ellie left, Claire tried to sleep. She was not deeply religious but knew abortion was out of the question for her. Even as she and Ellie had explored the possible options, it had never felt right. She had no qualms with what other people did in these situations, but she couldn't do it.

"Here I am, single, alone without Alan, and a baby who is a product of a horrible violent attack on the way. I hope I know what I'm doing."

She rolled over and dove under the comforter, never wanting to emerge again.

Chapter 5

Claire was dreaming of Alan again. Ever since the attack, he had come to her more frequently. She felt he was reaching beyond the grave; her own personal angel sent to let her know she wasn't alone. This time, it was like she'd had the power to stop time, to stay in a memory with him. To take in his handsome face and dancing eyes a little longer. Like she knew, as she sat there reliving a moment, that he was going to go. So she did everything she could to be there with him, to appreciate him, to look on him with all the love in her heart. She imparted it to him in big vibrations across the passenger seat as she envisioned him sitting there, driving.

They had just departed a dinner, where she had met Alan's brother Brian. The three of them had gotten on so well that Claire's heart was near to bursting as Alan took her home.

Suddenly she was in the restaurant as if she'd never left. Claire giggled as she sipped her Cabernet, and Alan poked fun at her anxiousness.

"So this is a surprise. Why don't you tell me more about Brian?" Claire smiled up into Alan's face, and his blue eyes softened as he peered back at her, a smile playing on his lips.

"Let's just say … he's a psychiatrist and younger than I am, but I'm better looking," Alan chuckled, and Claire pushed at his arm and laughed herself.

"That wouldn't be tough to accomplish, you sweet man," she purred at him, the wine making her feel loose and warm.

"You'll see, sweetheart." Alan winked and shot her another boyish smile.

Alan was an Irish rogue with wavy auburn hair and an easy manner. Freckles covered most of his face and arms, that Claire had once told him were angel kisses. "I'll connect the dots one day," she'd whispered after they'd made love the first time. He'd squeezed her a little tighter and nuzzled her hair, his muscular body a perfect fit to her frame. He was taller than she was and had a presence about him, the way he walked as if he knew he could handle business. Claire found that unbelievably sexy.

As soon as they'd started dating, he'd planned all their events, telling Claire that his ancestry necessitated he arrange all the parties. That, as a boy, he'd been forced to memorize all the Irish jokes. Although she often accused him of making some up! At that, Alan would hold up his palms and protest while laughing, "I swear on my grandpappy Duffy, that story's true." There was never a dull moment with him, yet he was so gentle and considerate. She admired that he knew his lineage, as she was a good ol' Heinz 57. Alan made sure to tease her about that, too. But it was always in good fun, resulting in her laughing right along with him, or rolling her eyes at him, and *then* busting a gut.

Part of her hoped that Brian would be so late that she could have Alan all to herself. In the dim lighting, his smile was brighter, his eyes darker, more violet than blue, and even more mysterious. She reached for his hand and rubbed her thumb over the top of it. He gave her a gentle squeeze back, then leaned over and kissed her. Claire felt her nerves ignite again. He still gave her butterflies even after months of dating.

As they waited for Brian to appear, Alan straightened up and signaled the waiter, who topped off Claire's glass.

"Are you trying to take advantage of me? Not that I'd object," Claire said.

"We never know what the night holds," Alan said with a bit of growl in his voice like he wanted to claim her right there—on top of the table. *Either that or the wine's going right to my head!*

Suddenly, Claire felt her eyes widen. A man had entered. He spoke for a minute with the hostess at the stand up front. She whipped her head from the man to Alan as Alan broke out in a deep laugh. That got the attention of the man who spotted Alan and sent a huge smile their way. Claire was smiling like a loon, too.

The man was headed toward them now, and he was *identical* to Alan. She ran her eyes up and down his body and all over his face, taking in his traits and then switching her study to Alan, who was still laughing, and now the man, Brian, was laughing, too.

"Brother," Alan said, rising from his chair and walking toward Brian, his arms outstretched.

"You didn't tell her, did you?"

"No, he did *not!*"

Now Claire was on her feet and holding her hand out to shake Brian's hand. Brian ignored her gesture and swept her into a hug, and she giggled, then pulled back and stared from one brother to the other.

"Oh, Alan," she laughed. "All this time, and there's two of you."

"Now, don't get any ideas," he chuckled.

"This is positively wonderful," Claire exclaimed as they all settled into their chairs at the table. "I guess when people say identical, this is what they mean!" She peered at the two of them slyly, "Are there *any* differences between the two of you—I mean ones you can mention?"

"Oh, she's got your number!" Brian said as Alan feigned a shocked look.

"I clearly have bigger feet," Alan boasted to more raucous laughter.

Dinner was a mix of lively conversation, bursts of laughter, a little too much wine, and savory food. Alan and Brian entertained her with childhood stories that one would start and the other would finish. After hours at the table and warning looks from the waitstaff, it was time to leave. They all said their goodbyes reluctantly, chatted about how important family is, and promised to do it again soon.

Then Alan and Claire were in the car, and it was as though she was there but not. She could see through Alan like a hologram. His image would flicker off and on, and Claire knew something was coming to take him away. He was going to leave her again. She wanted so badly to stay in the car with him.

Alan turned to her and said, "I love you, kiddo."

All she could do was smile back around the lump in her throat. It was raining, and the night was black; drops streaked past the windows, and dappled shadows played on Alan's face.

He was smiling as he drove, staring straight ahead as he said, "Don't get any ideas, cutie. Not only am I better looking, but I am a hell of a lot more fun, too." Claire sensed these were some of his last words, and her eyes filled with tears as she struggled to hold onto the happiness he always brought her.

"Oh, Al." She linked her arm through his and sidled closer to rest her head on his shoulder, taking in the scent of his cologne, loving all parts of him. His warm vanilla smell, the feel of his wool coat under her cheek, his low voice singing along to a slow ballad on the radio. "Let's just keep driving, all right," she whispered, "and never leave this car." An urgency in her heart tried so hard to grip onto the moment. If she held tight enough, maybe she wouldn't have to leave. Maybe she could hold him there, too. Claire glowed from the inside out as she fought a feeling of inevitable sorrow.

Then a car barreled toward them, heading the wrong way, its lights blinding them as Alan jerked the wheel to get off the road, but it was too late …

"Alan!" Claire sat bolt upright in bed, shuddering, breaking down. Her eyes darted all over the room until she realized it had all been a very real dream—as if she had been there with Alan in the car when he was killed. But in real life, when he had left this world, he had been alone.

Was he showing me his death?

As she had felt the rapture of their love in reliving her favorite moments, a deep grief knocked into her again. She gasped on her knees in the bed, rocking back and forth and hugging herself. "Why did you leave me?" She asked for the millionth time. *If you were here, I never would've gotten into this predicament. This would be your baby.*

Eventually, when dawn's rosy fingers tinged the windows, Claire had exhausted herself enough to roll over and pull the covers up to her chin. She slept until her alarm went off, and then, as she went about her morning getting ready for work, she told herself to concentrate on the blessings she and Alan had shared. It was work, but she pushed away the memory of the car racing toward them and Alan's desperate, remorseful voice telling her right before she woke up, "I'm so sorry, darling."

Instead, she gave thanks for the time she could spend with him in her dreams. And she even smiled later in the day when she recalled his warm blue eyes that always emanated such love for her.

"To be loved is so special," Claire whispered to herself as she waited at the copy machine for the collating to complete. "The way this is going, I don't think I'll ever love again."

It was a shocking revelation to herself that she would even think this way, but Claire was lonely and about to be a single mother. She gave herself a little grace as she leaned against the wall and listened to the whir of papers shuffling through the trays.

It's just you and me, kiddo, she thought at her unborn baby.

Chapter 6

Going to work each day presented challenges to Claire. The one saving grace was that her morning sickness occurred in the middle of the night or first thing in the morning before breakfast. She could usually get it over with and lurch her sweaty, teary-eyed self into the shower right after, then pull herself together.

"Good job, baby. Thanks for cutting me a break," she said, staring down at her naked belly. Then she smiled as she washed her hair and finished up.

Even though she tried to wear a happy face, the effort was wearing. Her frequent dreams of Alan, of re-experiencing the moment she'd learned he'd died—she'd never forget.

It had been a Thursday. She'd been stuck in a marketing meeting, discussing a client who kept changing direction. The gas station was trying to move from a Mom and Pop aesthetic, but whenever the design team came back with mock-ups, the owners reverted to their old identity. The team had called the meeting to hash out the best way to talk to the couple who owned the station and devise a plan for everyone to move forward.

Claire was exhausted, her head drooping, as she sat there and listened to Abby, the infamous droner, a copywriter on the team. Abby took over like she always did. No matter what idea was presented, Abby *always* had a problem with it. She paraded around the room, her blonde corkscrew curls bouncing, her eyes snapping behind blue cat-eye frames. Claire sank back in her seat and forced herself to listen, but she was thinking of her evening ahead with Alan. He was bringing over *The Godfather* movies, and they were going to watch them all over a series of days. Tonight was the first one. She could hear him in their recent conversation and swallowed back a smile as Abby prattled on.

"You're joking!" Alan had stared at her, his eyes round. "You've never … never seen any of these movies? These classic movies?" He dramatically draped a hand, palm-side up, across his eyes.

"No!" Claire covered her mouth with her hand and acted like she was ashamed of herself, sliding down the couch as Alan continued his mock horror routine.

"Well, it's been a good run," Alan said as he made to get up and leave. Claire grabbed him around the legs and pulled him onto the couch. *That was what—the twelfth time we'd done it?* Claire thought, tapping her finger on her lips, very aware she had better get it together. Abby disliked it when people didn't put all eyes on her when she was talking—or rather, giving orders. Claire forced herself to pay attention.

After another blessed half hour, the meeting had finally wrapped, and Claire retrieved her phone from her purse. She had fifty-three missed calls from Brian. She swayed on the spot as she collapsed into her chair. Her knees immediately started shaking, and all the breath went out of her as her jittering fingers dialed the phone. She didn't bother to listen to the voice mails.

Brian's voice wailed through the phone. "He's gone! Oh my God, my other half is gone! What am I—"

"Brian," Claire whispered through lips that felt like cinderblocks. Tears pricked her eyes. Her heart beat so hard she could feel it in her throat. "What are you saying? No, don't say it. Oh no, no, no, no, no …" All she could hear was a voice, a woman saying "no" fifty times, a hundred times. Then Vida and Ellie were there, and Claire was on her knees, her head on the seat of her chair, crying so hard; she didn't make a sound as tears rolled from her eyes. She didn't even realize she was crying; it was more like she was leaking and floating, and she had no idea where she was or who was saying what.

Vida spoke, "Claire, you've got to tell us what's wrong!" Her sharp tone pulled Claire up from the depths where she was drowning in a new dimension.

"Alan …" It was the weakest mewling sound leaving her mouth.

"What happened?" This was Ellie, crouching beside her, smoothing her hair back like she'd had too much to drink.

"Bri—he just said he's gone …"

"Where's the phone?" Vida took charge, her matter-of-fact voice still warm but leaving no doubt who was in charge.

Then …

"Brian? This is Vida, Claire's friend. What happened?"

Silence as Claire pinwheeled in and out of reality, desperately wanting to step back through time. She took a heaving breath and sobbed convulsively, somehow understanding, although she didn't know how to process it, that Alan was dead.

Vida was on the other side of her now.

"Alan was in a car accident," she said in the gentlest tone possible. "He died this afternoon. Claire, I am so sorry. I'll take you home. One of us will stay with you at all times until you can manage, okay?"

Claire lifted her soggy face off the chair and somehow managed to nod, and then Ellie and Vida had bundled her into one of their cars, Claire didn't know whose, and took her home.

There was a funeral, and details that when people are alive seem important, but when they're in the casket, no one cares. *Just honor him*, was all she thought as she discussed his arrangements. *I never learned Alan's favorite flower*. It was enough to send her into a paroxysm of sobbing again. She had been robbed and hadn't learned everything she'd wanted to about her precious Alan. There just hadn't been enough time. *Why God*, oh she was so angry as she railed thoughts heavenward. *If you were just going to take him away, why give him to me at all?*

That was enough remembering. She had to pull herself out of the past, jam her feet into low-slung heels, grab her bag, and head to work. "I hate you,

Hollingsworth," Claire hissed as the elevator took her to the parking floor.

It was incredibly challenging to keep her mind on work with Bryce's baby growing inside her. As the days went on, she felt a clock ticking and knew a lot of decisions that she didn't want to make had to be made. There was only so much time before she started showing and exhibiting signs of pregnancy that couldn't be ignored. She couldn't keep procrastinating.

One evening, as she browsed baby gear and clothes, she decided to call her sister, Chloe, better known as her rock. Chloe had tested the waters of life before Claire could get in. She had married first and had kids. Just through living, she showed Claire how to have it all. Claire loved her beyond measure.

Although they didn't live close, they were close—the distance didn't matter. Claire had dreaded telling Chloe about the rape and breaking her heart but figured if she could stay with Chloe, her husband Lou, and their two kids in their rambling Victorian house, maybe she could survive this unreality. Thank heavens, a plan was finally unfurling in her mind.

Chloe had plenty of room, and Claire was ready to pitch her new boss, who had taken Hollingsworth's place, about working remotely. Lots of people were doing it—especially her pregnant coworkers. It wasn't that she was ashamed of her baby. *It's not its fault the father was a deviant*, she always told herself. But she was freaked out about the timing of it all. Someone is sending me notes, *maybe knows something, and all of a sudden, I turn up pregnant—even though my fiancé is dead?* It didn't look good, and a twitch in her stomach warned against it. She had to leave town until the danger passed.

While she noodled on a story she could use to buy herself time to get through her pregnancy at Chloe's, Claire allowed herself to get a little excited about buying baby clothes and gear. She'd always wanted to be a mother as she loved children. *Just not this way . . .*

After checking out bassinets, onesies, a diaper service, and overpriced strollers, she let out a big breath, picked up the phone, and dialed Chloe. *Time to stop procrastinating.*

"Hey, sis!" Chloe's voice held a smile in it just for Claire.

Hearing her sister put a spark of joy in her heart immediately.

"Hi, I miss you," Claire blurted out.

Chloe laughed. "Me, too!" And then they were off, catching up and talking about kids and jobs and Lou, and laughing about all their adventures, until Claire interjected, "Clo, I need to stay with you, okay? Something major has come up, and I don't want to talk about it now, but I was hoping to come down, and tell you then. I mean, this would be months I'd be underfoot."

"Oh," Chloe said, and Claire thought she was holding back from grilling her about what was going on. Instead, she said, "Of course! As long as you want."

They decided she would come down at the first of the year. *If work lets me*, Claire ruminated, but she didn't tell Chloe that.

"Wait, you're not ill, are you?" Chloe asked.

"I sure hope not," Claire said and sent a smile back through the phone. "But seriously, it's nothing like that. Please don't worry."

After drawing out their goodbyes a little longer, the sisters eventually hung up. Claire sighed.

"Step one. Complete." She hugged her stomach.

"Step two. Convince the boss man." But that would have to wait until tomorrow. She headed back toward the bedroom to get to sleep early. As small as her baby was, it was sure wiping her out. For the first time in a long time, Claire thought everything might one day be okay. That night she didn't dream of Alan but of children playing in a ring around her.

Chapter 7

With plans to stay at Chloe's firmed up, Claire pondered different stories to use to explain wanting a leave of absence from work. After rolling around various options in her mind, she finally decided the best story, and hopefully the most believable, would be to say her sister needed her to help with the kids. Claire dreamed up that Chloe had to have surgery, her husband's job took him away from home, and she wouldn't feel comfortable with an outsider taking care of her kids.

It would have to do the trick as Claire couldn't think of anything better. It was critical that she stay out of sight and that her absence wouldn't be challenged too deeply. No polite person would think of asking why her sister was having surgery, and from what she knew of the new CEO, Everett Andrews, he was all about formalities.

This could work, Claire thought.

On the day she planned to approach Mr. Andrews, Claire selected a professional-looking navy blue suit, white-collared blouse, and low-heeled navy shoes. She wanted to give herself the best shot at him granting her wish.

Once she was dressed and had added button pearl earrings to her ensemble, she assessed her reflection and practiced various somber expressions.

Then she headed off for work.

As she sat at her desk reviewing a new account file that had been sitting in her inbox, she told herself there was no time like the present. *Just lay it all on the line*, she thought as she stood and pushed in her chair. Mr. Andrews had an open-door policy, where employees from all stations were always welcome to chat with him. Claire figured he would be in his office with the door slightly ajar. She was off to find out.

There was just one small problem. Her legs were shaking, her stomach was flipping—in a way that wasn't morning sickness—and she was breaking out in a sweat. The thought of being in the office where Bryce had presided made her unglued. She was terrified but forced herself to keep taking steps that led her closer to Mr. Andrews's office. *I need to do this, or staying here would be much more terrifying.* She couldn't get rid of the thought that her coworkers would put two and two together: Bryce's demise and her pregnancy. Logically, she knew that sounded ridiculous, but something was telling her to protect her baby. She wouldn't ignore that pang of motherly instinct—so she kept on walking.

At least she could comfort herself a little with the thought that she had only been in that office once before—when she had requested a leave of absence after Alan's accident.

Claire poked her head through the open door.

"Mr. Andrews? I'm sorry if I'm barging in. I know you always said anyone could come and see you …"

"Of course," Mr. Andrews boomed in his gruff voice. Claire thought of him as a mister even though he invited everyone to call him Everett. She just couldn't bring herself to address him any differently.

Mr. Andrews was a big man, not overweight but tall and well built. He wore a brown tweed jacket, cream-colored shirt, and blue print tie. His signature stylish glasses were round tortoiseshell frames. Claire wondered absently if his wife picked out his ties. *Or his glasses, for that matter.* She had loved picking out Alan's ties. It was a badge of honor in a relationship, like helping him shave or folding his laundry.

"Claire, what can I do for you?" Mr. Andrews asked. His voice was warm and smiley.

She was momentarily taken aback as she stood before him, resisting the urge to fidget like a child. It was just that the walls felt a little tighter than she remembered. The room looked the same: a huge oak desk and bookcase, and the same ugly plaid draperies with one exception—Bryce wasn't in it.

A flashback gripped Claire, and she remembered the feel of Bryce's rough hands on her wrists, the sound of his zipper, and his head thudding on the floor. Her heart pounded as Mr. Andrews waited for an answer.

Claire swallowed hard and forced herself to block the image and the sounds from her mind. Her voice was weak and whiny when she spoke, making her cringe all the more.

She cleared her throat. "I need to talk to you about something—a leave of absence, actually."

Mr. Andrews raised his eyebrows and steepled his fingers together. "Please have a seat." He gestured toward one of the two chairs facing him.

Claire scooted around to a chair and sat down.

"Tell me what you have in mind."

Oh, how she wanted to pour out the real reason she was there, to tell him that she was pregnant and worried. To ask him to please just believe that she hadn't done anything wrong, but of course, that was out of the question. Instead, she stammered out her lie. "I was hoping to take a leave right after the first of the year. My sister, Chloe, lives two hours south of here, and she needs my help." Claire looked down at her hands in her lap and willed herself not to pick her fingernails. She was horrified that she might start crying. Somehow, she lifted her head and babbled out more of the fabrication. "Unfortunately, she is going to require surgery. She and her husband have two small children, and her husband is away on business a lot of the time. She needs me to take care of the kids," Claire finished and blinked away the tears that had started forming.

Mr. Andrews took off his glasses and studied Claire carefully. "And how long would you be away?"

"About five or six months," Claire managed to get out while feeling her cheeks turn red.

"It would be that long?" Mr. Andrews asked as he polished his glasses on a little cloth he had retrieved from his desk drawer.

Claire knew that wasn't nearly long enough to get to the end of her pregnancy, but it was all she could dare to ask at that moment. She had to be careful that he wouldn't guess why she needed so many months away.

Mr. Andrews huffed on his glasses and made little circular motions with the cloth as he waited for Claire to answer. It was only a few seconds, but it felt like time had stopped.

"Yes, sir, sadly, the surgery is pretty major. My sister's doctor told her that she shouldn't do any lifting for five or six months." As she got her story straight, her voice gained strength—despite Mr. Andrews' steady eye contact. *There*, she thought, ashamed of the lie. *It's out in the open now.*

Mr. Andrews smiled gently at her and replaced his glasses. "There is a lot to be considered here. Would it be possible for you to work from your sister's home? I don't mind telling you, that's a huge factor in my decision."

"Yes, of course," Claire smiled back, sounding a little too eager, but from the look on Mr. Andrews's face, he didn't seem to notice.

He nodded at her and said, "All right, Claire. I will give your request consideration and get back to you."

Claire rose from the chair and smiled at him once more. "Thank you, Mr. Andrews. I will look forward to hearing from you." Then she darted out of the office before he could have a second thought and turn her down.

After two days and no word from Mr. Andrews, Claire was concerned.

If he denies my request, what will I do? As she waited for his response, she worked as hard as possible to ensure all he would hear about her performance was positive. Not that she didn't work hard every day and take extreme pride in her job and the quality of her work; she just put a touch more elbow grease into every task she was assigned.

Merely wondering what the end result would be was bad enough. Add on the thought that she would have to quit her job if she didn't get her request, and Claire was a mess.

Who else will hire a pregnant woman? Claire mused as she forced herself to pay attention to her work.

Wanting anything to take her mind off her worries, she asked Ellie and Vida to brunch at the Westin that coming Sunday.

Ellie chirped up that she couldn't wait for a little girl time. Vida was onboard, too. They all loved going to the fancy hotel and sipping mimosas as they noshed. *No mimosas for me. Vida is going to freak.*

Sunday came, and the girls gathered at a table. Ellie already had a fuzzy navel in her hand, and Vida was nursing a bloody Mary when Claire arrived. After a few minutes, the waiter came over and asked her what she would like to drink.

"Just a hot decaf tea, please," Claire said with a smile.

"What?" Vida burst out. "You're not having anything stronger than tea? I thought this was a party!" She nailed Claire with a suspicious look, one eyebrow hiked up on her forehead. "What's going on, miss?"

Claire and Ellie exchanged a glance, as Claire slowly said, laying her hand on Vida's, "Don't make a big deal out of this, okay? But I am not drinking alcohol for a very good reason." Claire rushed on, thinking briefly how she had gotten into the habit lately of springing surprises on people. "I have something to tell you, and I should have told you earlier. But the reason I didn't is because I was petrified of this news getting out."

"You better spit it, girl." Vida crossed her arms and erased all emotion from her face.

"Fine, but the only reason I told Ellie was because I was about to explode with all that's happened to me, and I couldn't handle it alone anymore, and I should have said—"

"If you don't get to the point—" Vida pouted.

"I know I can confide in you, but I was just so panicky. Please don't be mad at me—"

"I will be if you don't stop dragging this out. But really, what's going on? Are you okay?"

"I'm pregnant, but that's the best part of the news. The other part is pretty awful." Ellie nodded and placed a hand on Claire's arm.

Then, with a shake in her voice, Claire recounted all the details of the night Bryce assaulted her.

Claire could see by the shock in Vida's eyes that she was aghast.

Her shock soon gave way to empathy as she rushed to Claire's side and swept her up in a hug. As she pulled back, tears stood out in Vida's eyes. She swiped them away. "He's lucky he's dead, or I would have finished the job!" Anger had replaced Vida's fleeting sadness. Claire knew her friend well. With her feisty attitude and take-no-bullshit stance in life, Vida wanted revenge.

"No, Vida," Claire shook her head. "He didn't deserve to die, and I am the one responsible for his death!" Vida crushed Claire again in a hug, then returned to her chair. "I still can't forgive myself," Claire whispered.

The waiter dropped off her drink and three plates just then and told the trio to go load up at the buffet. At the sight of him, Claire clammed up and sipped her tea to settle her nerves.

After they had filled their plates and gotten fresh drink refills, Claire filled Vida in on her talk with Mr. Andrews.

"Now, here it is the weekend, and I still don't know if he's going to approve my leave. If he doesn't, I have to find another job. I just couldn't stay there. Maybe no one would figure it out, but they sure would know I'm pregnant, and I don't know, a part of me just wants to keep that to myself." A tear rolled down Claire's cheek, and she dabbed it with her cloth napkin as Vida's and Ellie's faces softened. "What if someone asks about the father of the baby? They know Alan just died. They'll think I'm easy, and I'll have to lie again. The one lie I had to tell Mr. Andrews was bad enough!"

"But there's another bombshell if you can stomach it," Claire told her friends as Vida's eyebrow did its thing again.

"I'm pretty full up, and I just had that popover, but okay," Vida said with a sly smile. And Claire knew she was trying to cheer her up and reassure her by talking about normal things.

At that, Claire let Vida in on the notes she'd received and how she had no idea who was sending them.

Ellie appeared sad again as she swirled lemon water around in her tumbler, and once more, fury danced in Vida's eyes.

"Let's figure out who the hell it is then," Vida declared and knocked back the rest of her drink. She plucked a pickle spear out of her empty glass and took a bite. "Ellie, you know who the first person was who encountered the rat bastard's body. Who was it again?"

Ellie's brow crinkled as she tried to remember all the details that had rushed out in the aftermath of Bryce's death. "I remember now! Oh my God, it was Scotty!" She looked a little triumphant as she sat back in her chair with a grin.

Vida was immediately convinced they'd found the culprit. "That pitiful weasel worm," she shrieked as Claire held a finger to her lips.

But Vida would not be silenced. "How dare he try and pull a stunt like this! What's the purpose? Blackmail? Money? Sex?" Vida's face flushed as she hit on each new idea for what would drive Scotty to send the notes.

"We don't know it's him," Ellie interjected in the middle of Vida's ranting.

Vida ignored her and said, "I'll take care of him. Have no doubt. I'll crush his little extortions, and if he doesn't cooperate, that's not all I'll crush." To prove her point, Video popped two green olives in her mouth and bit down hard. Claire and Ellie giggled as Vida stared back with a closed-mouth grin and finished chewing.

"Okay, Godzilla," Claire chuckled. "What do you have in mind?" *It will feel good to put this nonsense behind me and get Scotty—if that's who it is—under control.*

"Let's just say an idea is forming and that lowlife will never harass you again. It's a good thing I'm PMS'ing right now. I can take it out on him!"

"Ooh, watch out!" Ellie pointed her fork at Vida, who laughed and tried to snatch it.

"She's gonna blow!" Claire laughed. Then her smile slid off her face, and tears replaced her grin at her friend's antics. "You guys are just the best," she said. This time both girls rose and shared a group hug.

"Musketeers," Ellie said with a weepy smile. "All of this will be fixed before you know it!"

"Yeah," Claire said teasingly, "then maybe we can put Ms. Beast mode away."

"Perhaps …" Vida smiled, but Claire knew once Vida latched onto an idea, or someone she loved had been hurt, she didn't let up.

That thought was comforting and terrifying at the same time. *Just how much does Scotty know? Has he already gone to the police? Is that why the radio silence from Mr. Andrews?*

Once again, Claire's mind was twisting about as fast as her stomach.

Chapter 8

"Hello, Scotty, how's it going?" Vida inquired with the most winning smile she could muster.

"Oh, actually, okie-dokie!"

Vida ignored his dorkiness; she looked him up and down like she was skimming a menu. "I was wondering if maybe the two of us could get together after work someday? For a drink?" Secretly she thought, *unless chocolate milk is the strongest drink you can handle?*

"Sure, I guess ..." Vida sensed suspicion in Scotty's eyes. "What's up? You've never wanted to spend time with me before. Why now?" Scotty pressed.

Vida broadened her smile and said, "It's a big secret, but I really would love to share it with you." She pretended to find some lint on his shirt and pluck it off Scotty's stiff body. He didn't seem like he was breathing. She got a little closer, enjoying watching him squirm. "And I think you *really* need to hear it."

Scotty regained the ability to breathe. His eyes widened as he stammered, "Whoaaa-wow! Now you have my curiosity whetted."

It would be best to meet at least a couple of blocks away from the office. "How about the bar at Tortoise?" Vida suggested. "It's quiet. Do you know where that is?"

"Never heard of it."

"Well, it's easy to find. Gimme your phone, and I'll put the address in."

Scotty handed it over, and Vida punched in the info.

"Tonight at seven, or is that too late for you?"

Scotty flashed a quick scowl at her. "I can make it," he said acidly.

"See you tonight," Vida said, swallowing back the urge to leer at him one last time before she dropped the bomb on him later.

Vida arrived at the restaurant first, and found a nice quiet spot for their conversation. The hostess, wearing a high-waisted apron and carrying a glass water carafe and wine glasses between her fingers, led her to a booth in the corner. Vida scooted across the bench, removed her black puffer coat, and picked up the menu.

She wasn't there more than three minutes when she spied Scotty walking toward her. He wore a heavy winter jacket and looked even more infantile. *As if that's possible.*

Vida waved to him, and he strolled over—obviously in no hurry to join her.

Boy, this is going to be good, Vida thought.

The waitress came over, and Vida ordered a white wine. Scotty flipped through the menu a couple of times, then decided on a draft beer.

The waitress walked away, and they exchanged a few words about the cold weather until their drinks arrived.

"Cheers," Scotty said and raised his glass. Vida raised hers to his and clinked.

"Vida," Scotty said out of a shit-eating grin, "This is such a surprise. A pleasant one, I might add. What's the occasion?"

"Let's see …" Vida then narrowed her eyes and lowered her voice. "I understand you have been very busy sending little notes, no signature, and no return address to Claire. Isn't that true?"

Scotty's face reddened. "I don't know what you're talking about." He dropped his eyes to his drink.

Now Vida drilled her finger into the table, bam, bam, bam! She smiled, but it was more peeling her lips off her teeth as if she was smile-snarling at him. "But I think you do. My friend Claire has been receiving these notes, and she has absolutely no idea what this is all about. So don't bullshit me."

Scotty slouched back in his chair like he wanted to slide under the table. "What made you zero in on Claire, anyway? Was it because of the initial 'C'?" She started laughing, little giggles bubbling out of her throat. "Because you are so off base, you're playing a different game. You're in a different stadium all the way across town."

Scotty scowled. "There's more to it than that." He took a swig of his beer that appeared oversize in his small hand. He patted his mouth with a napkin, resembling a mouse as he did so—he was the mere vermin torturing her friend. "It's not only the initial. I saw Hollingsworth eyeing Claire at the party. Every time I looked at him, he was staring at her."

"What were you doing checking him out all night long?"

"It's not like that," Scotty said, his voice cracking. "I admit," he said, wagging his finger at Vida, "I couldn't figure out why her compact would be in the men's room. Seemed to me he was interested in her."

"I admire your commitment to playing such a role," Vida said as she rolled her eyes. "But I've had enough. Now, it's time to fill you in." Vida leaned back and crossed her arms, leveling him with what she hoped was a scathing look. At that moment, she hated him so much that she felt herself grow hot in her sweater. Her palms were suddenly clammy. Loathing oozed out of her pores. As she considered it, hating Scotty wasn't a leap, but he represented something more than just his dumb game. Scotty was evil. Vida could sense that. He sent all the hair on the back of her neck on end, and beneath her emotional swagger was the feeling she couldn't stand: fear. Scotty made her want to spin her head around and ensure they weren't alone in the restaurant. *No way in hell will I walk with him to our cars.*

She gathered her composure and ordered her voice to be steady as she said, "Are you sure you're harassing the right person?" Scotty's expression didn't change. He was now attempting to look bored as he fidgeted with a hangnail.

Vida took in a big breath and blew it out. "Scotty, Scotty, I am going to tell you a little story that I want you to keep strictly between us. I hope I can count on you to keep a secret."

Scotty couldn't respond fast enough. "Of course, Vida. Just between the two of us, scout's honor." He held up his hand like he was taking an oath.

Vida cleared her throat. "I knew it was wrong with him being married and all, but he was just so damned handsome and sexy, I just couldn't resist." She hung her head like the affair was so heavy it curved her back.

"Are you trying to tell me you cheated with a married man?"

"I'm afraid that's the naughty truth," sighed Vida.

"Why are you telling me this?" Scotty peered at her. "Wait!" He held a finger up as if he'd suddenly remembered the answer to a long-forgotten question. "Is it someone I know?"

Vida scoffed. "Scotty! Follow the train of thought here. Who were we talking about before my confession?"

"Huh!" Scotty inhaled so quickly, he squeaked.

"That's right," Vida said. "Let me connect the dots. It *was* Bryce Hollingsworth."

"You're not kidding?" Scotty asked.

Vida's gaze dropped to her hands for a few seconds. She lifted her eyes slowly to meet him as if she was ashamed. "It's the truth. The last time we were together was the afternoon before the big party. My purse was too small to hold my makeup, car keys, and everything else, so I asked Bryce to keep my compact for me 'til next time. He put it into his suit jacket. It must've slipped out when he fell."

Scotty appeared more confused than usual like he was trying to decide if he should believe Vida.

She charged on, not as afraid of him as much since he was unraveling, "By the way, the 'C' is for Cabello, my last name."

That removed the final doubt from Scotty's mind. Vida could see it all over his face. He leaned forward and laced his fingers together.

"Scotty, I know I can trust you to keep this affair to yourself. No one needs to know, especially now. It would only cause hard feelings … and … please, I don't want to lose my job."

Scotty nodded woodenly.

"When things like this get out, you suddenly find yourself on the other side of someone else's agenda to kick you to the curb! Please, Scotty." Vida forced tears to well up in her eyes.

Now Scotty gave her a victorious smile.

"I thought you would play hardball," Vida nodded a few times like she was sizing him up. She turned her tears off instantly and glared at him. "To ensure that you keep this to yourself, I want you to know I've been watching you."

The smile slid off Scotty's face.

"I have seen you take money out of the jar at the coffee station. You always check to be sure no one is around, then ever so quickly, pick up the money and jam it into your pants pocket. Did you really think no one would find out?"

Scotty reached for his beer, and Vida laid a hand over his, the bile nearly rising in her throat at touching him. "Silly you. But don't worry. This offense isn't a police matter."

He yanked his pudgy hand away as Vida went on, "The embarrassment would be just as bad, though. It might even cause you to lose your job."

Vida caught her reflection in the floor-to-ceiling mirror across the room, and saw her eyes sparkle with accusation. *I'd watch my step around me*, she thought, and had to curtail a laugh.

"So, Scotty, what did you intend to do with your information about the compact? Were you angling for money—oh, I forgot, I should say more money. Or maybe it was sex? Was that it? Did you want Claire to sleep with you?" Now she did laugh.

Scotty didn't answer her, but tried to explain himself.

"It was an odd find and near the body. I don't know. I just picked it up and walked off with it. And no, not sex. I was gonna figure it out eventually, but writing the notes—my head just told me to do it, I 'spose." He paused a minute. *Like he's trying to cook up some sincerity.* "Not money, either."

"Then spit it out, pipsqueak!"

"I will. I am! It's complicated … I'm from Kokomo, Indiana, and Lucy, my longtime girlfriend, my high school sweetheart, actually, still lives there. Someday, hopefully, we'll live there together. In the meantime, I live here with my aunt, Florence, but I travel every other week to see her."

"Gas money," Vida sputtered. "This is about *gas money?* You are hurting *my friend* who never did a damn thing to you because your lazy ass can't make enough gas money?"

"The trip takes me just under three hours one way—"

"That's no reason to torment someone!"

"It's not gas money. It's love, you dumbass!"

"You don't want to go there with me, dude!" Vida fought back the urge to scream at him.

"I want to be with her as often as I can, and my aunt's a complete tightwad. She's got money but won't give me any. She even tells me not to ask her for it anymore."

"You think she owes you?" Vida couldn't believe this moron.

"She doesn't do anything. Just sits around every day, and she is loaded!"

"I feel sorry for her with a nephew like you!"

Scotty's expression changed again then. His eyes darkened to a deep brown, bordering on black. His face was stone. Vida wondered where he went or if he was in a trance.

He gave a little jolt like someone had poked him under the table and picked up right where he left off, not missing a beat. "My aunt charges me rent, which strips my income down to nothing, *and* she makes me pay to *park* there. There's nothing left of my paycheck, and then I spend the rest on Lucy."

"You truly don't have a heart or a brain. Are we in Oz?" Vida snapped.

"I'm not a thief, Vida. And I am really ashamed of taking the money from the jar. I promise it will never happen again." He paused and leaned in a little closer as Vida backed away. "Anyway," Scotty lightened his tone, "tell me about the compact."

Vida sighed and said, "It's a lovely story concerning a family tradition, a quinceañera, and it signifies a girl leaving her childhood and becoming a woman on her fifteenth birthday. The party is always lavish, and the girl being honored wears a formal gown. On mine, I was showered with gifts and well-wishes. We had lots of food, music, and an all-around celebration."

"I've heard of that," Scotty nodded.

"Okay—so one of the gifts I received was that beautiful compact with my initial. Remember 'C' for Cabello? My parents gave it to me, so you can see how special it is." Scotty was hanging on like he'd been snagged on a fishing line.

Boy, I'm almost too good at spinning these wild tales. She and the girls would have a good laugh about it later.

"I get it," Scotty said. "I don't have it on me, but I'll return it to you tomorrow morning first thing."

"Thank you, Scotty. I can't wait to get it back and have been sick with worry over what happened to it." Scotty nodded reverently, a hollow gesture. "No one said anything about it, not even when they removed Bryce's body. I thought that was strange …" Vida said in a reflective tone. "Then I was panicked, figuring it was gone forever."

While she lied her head off, she couldn't help thinking how great it would be to hand the compact over to Claire.

They parted ways shortly after that. Vida made sure to linger back at the restaurant, pretending she needed to use the restroom for a good, long time.

No way will I be stuck with that weirdo, she shuddered.

Chapter 9

The next day at work, after everyone had settled in for the morning, Vida casually walked to Claire's desk, the look on her face like the cat that had swallowed the canary—all smiles and happy mischief.

"Good morning, Claire," she practically purred. "How is everything going?"

Claire glanced up, a little startled. "Vida!" She grinned at her friend. "All okay, I guess. You?"

Vida ignored her question. "I have a surprise for you!" Her amber eyes danced.

"Oh?" Claire questioned.

"Yes!" Vida clapped. "It's something that will make your smile even broader."

Hardly able to contain herself, Vida reached into her jacket pocket and produced the compact. She handed it to Claire, whose eyes flew open.

"Goodness, Vida! How in the world did you get that from Scotty?"

Vida gave her a wink and a nod and said, "Easy peasy, kiddo. I'll fill you in later."

Unbeknownst to Claire and Vida, Scotty watched the exchange and thought to himself, *why would Vida give the compact to Claire?* As he stared at Vida walking away, the compact still securely with Claire, his face grew hot. *Her story was all bullshit? That bitch!*

He clenched his fists, his thoughts boiling over again. *There will be payback.*

Later that morning, Mr. Andrews stopped by Claire's desk and asked her to follow him to her office. Claire jumped up and trailed behind him, hoping the news was good, that she could focus on packing up and leaving for her sister's.

She couldn't deny the pit in her stomach that she hoped meant nothing. If he turned down her request, she didn't have a plan B. It just had to work!

After they entered his office, Mr. Andrews pointed to the door and said, "Close it, please?"

Claire shut the door, her knees quaking. She turned around, and Mr. Andrews indicated a chair across from his desk. "Have a seat." He smiled slightly as she rushed over and sat down, her heart pounding. Despite her burgeoning fear that he would reject her request, she plastered on a smile and sent it his way.

"Well, Claire," he began. His face held an expression Claire couldn't figure out. All she could do was sit primly, knees together, fingers laced, on the edge of her seat. He continued in a warm tone, "I have turned your request over and over in my mind, and I am very hopeful that we can accommodate you."

Claire let out a big breath, and Mr. Andrews chuckled. "Little worried, were you?"

"No," Claire laughed. "Well, yes, I guess. I'm sorry. Please continue."

"I'm counting on you to hold up your end of the bargain. You said you can still carry your workload even with your additional responsibilities?"

His smile was so warm and welcoming. He was so different than Mr. Hollingsworth. *But you can't let your mind go there!* She ordered herself and instead answered, "Absolutely! I will work every day, and you won't even know I'm not physically here. There won't be an interruption in the workload, I promise. Everything will be the same, but just from home."

"Wonderful, Claire, we'll give it a try. I do hope you can return to the office earlier than you indicated. Do you think you can try?"

"I'll do my best, sir." Claire rose from her chair. "Thank you."

Mr. Andrews stated, "I believe you noted you would like to leave right after the first of the year."

"Yes, that is correct—if that is agreeable with you, of course."

"Fine, fine," he waved a beefy hand in her direction. "I will take care of the necessary paperwork, so you will be all set to begin working remotely on January second of next year. Gotta take some time to celebrate—and recover from the New Year!" He smiled once more in a manner that made Claire squirm in a good way. "I must tell you … I do admire you for stepping in to help your sister and her family. Very commendable."

"Thank you, sir," Claire blurted, her cheeks red.

He put out his hand for a handshake, and Claire stood up and allowed her dainty palm to be swallowed up by his. At the door, she waggled her fingers briefly at him, then stepped outside.

As she passed Ellie's and Vida's desks, Claire winked at each of them.

With her leave official, Claire sat at her desk and mentally composed a to-do list. At the top of her list was making an appointment with her doctor. She knew it was early in her pregnancy, and she hadn't had a doctor even confirm it yet, but there was no doubt in her mind. She had her positive tests and the symptoms.

Now the wheels were turning. She was truly going forward with her plan to leave the office and begin this next phase of her life—raising a child. If she let her mind wander on that topic too long, she got overwhelmed. *No*, she told herself, *you are not going down those crazy roads. Stay on task!*

Claire returned to the work waiting for her on her desk and decided she'd better get busy and get ahead while she could.

If Mr. Andrews walks by my desk and sees me sitting and thinking of God knows what, he may change his mind about my leave.

As she leafed through the pages of the agency's latest proposal—a new cleaning product—it was nearly impossible to concentrate on what she was reading.

"Pull yourself together! You have work to do!" she hissed in a barely audible whisper. She did her best to brainstorm a way to market the product, but her mind kept wandering, like a spool of thread unwinding.

And so the day went. Claire's mind kept returning to her baby and all the preparations that needed to be made.

Finally, five o'clock arrived, and she hauled herself out of her chair. Beyond exhausted, she gathered her things and headed home.

Once safely inside her front door, she heaved a giant sigh of relief. Now she could fully surrender to her mind racing. She sloughed off her jacket, purse, and laptop bag, kicked off her shoes, and immediately made a call to her OBGYN to schedule her first official appointment. Luckily, her doctor could squeeze her in in the next two days.

Hooray! One hurdle down, ten million to go, or so it seems.

Claire took her hair down as she walked back to her bedroom. There, she changed into her sweats. She could feel herself start to relax. In the kitchen, she reached for a bottle of wine before stopping herself and chuckling. A glass of water would have to do.

Water in hand, Claire walked back to her bedroom and stood in front of her full-length mirror. She lifted up her shirt and stared at her stomach to see if it was protruding.

Her cheeks went red as she studied her reflection. There was no bump yet, but she wouldn't have to wait long.

No matter how silly she told herself it was, one thought nagged at the back of her mind.

Will anyone at the office count up the time frame and connect the dots, believing I had anything to do with Bryce's death?

It was so ridiculous she couldn't help but laugh at herself. Still, she was afraid. *Any murderer would be,* she chided herself.

That was her thought cycle now—thinking of the insane possibilities and trying to talk herself out of them. She wasn't entirely convinced that the timeline wouldn't be a worry.

Paranoid much?

Claire stepped away from the dresser, her shirt now properly in place.

Nothing will ever come of that day, she reassured herself, willing herself to believe it. *But now I have problems.* She stood in front of the mirror once more. *Problems as big as the blue whale I'll look like at the end of my pregnancy.*

A remote part of her mind recognized that she wasn't being nice to herself, but she couldn't help it. She wasn't proud of her situation even as her conscience argued it wasn't her fault.

Her attention snapped back to the baby and everything that needed to be done. All the minutiae made her think of Alan. *He was always so good with details.* She had depended on him so much in that area and had worked so hard to think more like him lately.

Claire grabbed her glass of water off the nightstand and returned to the living room. She pulled her laptop out of her computer bag, settled on the couch, and surfed for baby products.

The list of things to buy was endless at Buy Buy Baby, but Claire had to admit that she loved shopping for all the tiny clothes. By the time she finished putting everything in the cart she could possibly think of that a baby would need, she'd run up quite the bill. Thankfully shopping online gave her a little anonymity since her packages would be delivered to her apartment. She wouldn't be seen around town loading up a huge cart and be at risk of someone she knew spotting her. *God forbid, maybe even a coworker!*

Then the phone rang, and all baby thoughts went out the window.

"Hi, Claire. It's Ellie. How about coming over to my place for a visit? Let's order pizza—if that sounds good. I thought I would call Vida, too. What do you say?" There was a slight pause and then Ellie's pleading voice. "Please say yes."

"Sounds great, Ellie! I haven't even thought about dinner. What time?"

"An hour okay?"

"Perfect," Claire said and genuinely smiled. She loved her friends and was starting to get used to the idea of a new normal. Every day when she woke up, she tried to push aside the dark thoughts that, if she let them, would take her down. She couldn't change what had happened, and it made more sense to pretend it was far away than to dwell on it. Maybe one day she could stomach all the facts, but for now, she was moving ahead in her mind and through her actions.

Forty-five minutes later, Claire was knocking on the door of Ellie's apartment.

When Ellie opened the door, they exchanged hugs. Over Ellie's shoulder stood a beautiful Christmas tree in front of expansive windows. Ellie's apartment was on the second floor of an old warehouse that had been converted into apartments. The decor was minimalist mid-century modern, and fit Ellie all the way down to her clothes. Ellie made upscale comfort a lifestyle. A beige shag rug covered most of the floor, and every table and flat surface boasted framed photos of her family.

Ellie released Claire from their hug, and Claire smiled at her friend. "Your tree is so pretty. I haven't even been thinking about the holidays. There's so much on my mind, and I can't wait to hear everything that's been going on with you and Vida."

Ellie smiled at Claire in a warm, knowing way as she grabbed a hot chocolate for her. They settled into the living room, Ellie on the couch, one leg folded underneath her, Claire curled up in a chair.

Vida arrived a few minutes later, and after more hugs, smiles, and a warm greeting, the ladies all sat down with drinks. Ellie and Vida stuck to wine.

Claire said, "Well, should I go first, or do one of you have some big news?"

Vida waved her hand in Claire's direction and said, "I am perfectly content to focus on you ... and this wine. What did Mr. Andrews say about your leave?"

They all laughed, then Claire took a deep breath and said quickly, "Right now, that is the most important news on my plate." Ellie and Vida leaned forward as Claire continued, "He said yes." Her two friends smiled at her and gave each other air high fives. Claire laughed a little and said, "But he feels the time frame is a little long and wants me to think about shortening it." Claire stirred her hot chocolate. "Obviously, that can't happen."

Ellie gave her a reassuring smile. "Don't worry about that! You'll be able to stay the required time. Mr. Andrews is such a wonderful man. He'll come around to agreeing to the time you need."

Vida nodded vigorously. "Ellie is right. You know that, Claire. Try not to worry. That's the last thing you need to deal with. In fact, it's pretty damn beneficial to remain calm right now."

"Easier said than done," Claire said, then scooped up a marshmallow and ate it, savoring the sweet gooeyness. "By the way, Vida," Claire gestured with her spoon at Vida, "Did you let Ellie in on the compact saga? If not, can you please fill in the blanks? I just want to chill versus talk right now. And don't leave out how you got him to hand it over without him asking why. That's the best part."

Vida smiled a broad and somewhat mischievous smile. "It was quite easy.

I told him it was my compact, given to me by my parents on my fifteenth birthday. The story was all the more believable because I have the same last initial as your first initial."

"Smart!" Ellie said.

Claire pressed, "But how did you explain your compact being in the men's room? You never told me that part this morning."

Vida took a slug of wine and announced, holding her glass aloft, "I told Scotty that Bryce and I were having an affair."

Claire wanted to laugh and brush the nightmare memory off, but she forced herself to smile and wait for Vida to finish.

"Scotty's so gullible and young. I told him that Bryce and I had been together the afternoon before the party—if you get my drift—and I had asked Bryce to hold my compact because I didn't have enough room in my bag."

"Sometimes the hardest circumstances require the easiest explanations," Ellie said, right before the doorbell rang.

When the pizza arrived, Claire realized she was hungrier than she realized. The girls continued chatting and eating. Time flew by until they reluctantly discussed calling it a night.

Vida got up and looked out the window, then turned to Claire. "It's still snowing, but the streets are only wet. Nothing's sticking. Did you drive?" Claire stood and joined Vida to study the streets below.

"No, I walked, and I better break up this party if I'm going to get home before the snow buries me."

"You'll do no such thing." Vida put an arm around Claire and smiled at Ellie. "Besides, Ellie would kill me if I let you freeze to death. You're coming with me. I'll drop you off. It's only a few blocks out of the way."

Claire gave her a small smile and went to grab her coat. As she pulled it on, she turned toward Vida and said, "I really can't thank you enough. Not just for the ride. For getting my compact back."

Vida bared her teeth in a funny grin. Claire chuckled and said, "Seriously, Scotty zeroed in on the idea it was mine. No telling what crazy ideas he has in his head."

"Or what he'll do about them," Ellie muttered almost as an afterthought as Claire and Vida made their way to the door.

Claire shivered. Ellie looked at her pointedly, wiping off any worry from her face. She gave Claire a hopeful look. "Nothing but a weird memory now," Ellie said as she lingered in the doorway seeing Claire and Vida out.

Chapter 10

The snow didn't amount to much overnight, and Claire chatted with Vida and Ellie in between working. She made sure to stay on task, knowing now was not the time to slack with Mr. Andrews keeping a closer eye on her. Her plan was at stake, and she would not fail herself or the little blueberry in her belly.

After the work day wrapped up, she bid Vida and Ellie goodbye through a stifled yawn. Then she headed home, grateful that she could finally relax and rest a little. The pregnancy made her very tired, and she had to resist falling asleep at her desk.

∽

Vida was one of the last out the door, and she made the short walk to the parking garage, her heels clicking on the pavement. *Brrrr, freezing!* She thought as she jogged as fast as she could in her pumps. The cold cut through her, the air feeling nearly wet. She unlocked the door, ready to slide behind the wheel and wait for the heat to kick on. But then her eye caught something, and her heart sank—a flat tire on the rear driver's side. She did slide behind the wheel then, but only to start the car, shivering in the cold, before punching in the number for AAA she'd retrieved from her insurance card in her glovebox.

An hour later, with a fresh tire on her car and at least a little thawed out, Vida steered toward home. The question kept plaguing her. *Where did that flat come from?* She'd only bought new tires a few weeks ago. It was something that everyone did in Chicago. Right as winter hits, you put on your snow tires. She could still hear her dad coaching her on that when she got her first car at sixteen.

The next day at work was a repeat of the day before—in *all* ways. When Vida walked to her car at five o'clock, she noticed this time that the back right tire was flat. The day before, it had been the left. Chiding herself that she was being silly, she'd walked to the right side of the car to check out the tire and make sure she was in tip-top shape to drive home. And it was weird, but she felt this time that someone was watching her. *Maybe I was spied on yesterday, too.*

The day before had been much colder, and in trying to escape the whipping wind she hadn't given much thought to who might be out there in the deserted garage with her. The hair rose on the back of her neck—not from the wind, but a suspicion. She scrambled to open the driver's side door and dove behind the wheel, slamming the door behind her and smashing down the lock with trembling fingers.

Her breath hung in the air as she entered the same number she'd called yesterday into her phone. She chuckled with the agent on the other end of the line at AAA, making bad jokes about her misfortune. Underneath, icy terror gripped her. *Something is so wrong. Who the hell did I offend and why do they want to do this to me, or worse?*

Another forty-five minutes later and Vida headed for home, the streetlights highlighting the gray, drizzly night. Finally, she could unclench her shoulders from her ears and force herself to breathe as normally as possible. She changed the record in her head. *No more being afraid.* Instead, she would think of Christmas and getting home to spend time with her grandma. She would envision the feast laid out on the table, the scents rising from the steaming homemade dishes. She would remember the giggles of her little nieces and nephews as they roughhoused around the tree that emanated the tangy fragrance she adored.

Stepping back in time helped chase away the heebie-jeebies. Before she knew it, she was pulling into her condo garage, the eerie mood of the night forgotten.

By daybreak, the fire in Vida's belly was back. She was never one to lie down and let someone make her fearful. It went against the very core of who she was.

Now she was torn. Christmas was quickly approaching, and she was leaving for Mexico with her parents to spend Christmas with her grandmother. But after last night and the night before, she had mixed feelings about leaving. The mystery of *why* or if someone was trying to scare her haunted her.

In the end, she decided it was best to get out of town for a while. *The person slashing my tires must be loco. I'll leave it at that for now.*

※

Ellie was thinking about the holidays, too. She had invited her parents and a few friends for Christmas dinner. As a Scandinavian—the last name of Nilsson gave her away—she often daydreamed of traveling to Sweden to learn more about her ancestry. She had seen pictures of the country houses, with their red painted roofs against backgrounds of rolling verdant hills and deep blue streams. Everything looked so peaceful and clean. People didn't call her "svenska flicka," which translated to "Swedish girl," for nothing.

She loved entertaining and planning a menu for her family and friends. This Christmas, she opted for a traditional Swedish meatballs appetizer, and some cheese and crackers.

Ellie had invited Claire, of course, and although Claire had received a couple of other invitations from friends, she was happy to go to Ellie's. When Claire walked through Ellie's door, the familiar aromas of something delicious roasting in the oven hit her square in the nose.

Ellie had soft Christmas music playing, and with the house decorations, Claire decided the scene resembled a ***House Beautiful*** magazine cover. Throughout the evening, Claire enjoyed visiting with Ellie's parents, her boyfriend Joe, and other friends and family members. The dinner was exceptional: ham, turkey, mashed potatoes and gravy, lingonberries, fresh carrots, Swedish butter cookies, and ice cream for dessert—accompanied by the endless pouring of hot black coffee.

A wonderful Christmas day was enjoyed by all, and the festivities did a world of good to keep Claire's mind occupied with joy, love, and a full stomach. Ellie was satisfied that all her work for the day had turned out so well.

When the guests were leaving, she walked over to Claire and, laying her hand on her shoulder, said, "I am so happy you decided to spend the day here with the people I am closest to. It was good to get your mind off other things." She smiled gently.

Claire smiled back, her heart instantly warmed by Ellie, who loved nothing more than taking care of everyone around her.

"Oh, Ellie, I can't thank you enough. This night was exactly what I needed and the best gift of all." Claire squeezed Ellie. "The only person missing was Vida."

"Yes," Ellie nodded. "I was going to invite her, but she told me how big of a day Christmas is for her and her family. I'm happy she's with everyone again. She missed her family so much. Trust me. I know how lucky I am."

"I'm lucky, too, friend," Claire said, unknotting her scarf from around a coat tree. "And I'll be lucky to get ahead of this snowstorm."

Claire gave Ellie one more hug and darted out the door.

☙

Vida was enjoying her Christmas in Mexico. She was happy to see her grandmother still honoring all the Mexican Christmas traditions Vida had enjoyed her entire life. As she walked into her grandma's house, the sights and smells instantly transported her to when she was a little girl, all excited for Christmas, presents, and the food made with so much love by all her aunties. A large nativity was set up in a place of honor in the living room, as a small Christmas tree glowed and a few poinsettias anchored the base of the tree.

Vida took in the whole scene, smiled, and waved around the room at all her relatives gathered. Then she turned toward her grandma, standing there with her arms outstretched. She walked into the older woman's embrace. "What's for dinner, Grandma? As if I didn't know," joked Vida. Her grandma spanked her and laughed along with everyone else.

Vida pulled back and grinned into her grandma's twinkly eyes. "Is it tamales, as always, with an ensalada and all the usual fruits and vegetables? Do you think Papá Noel will show up? Shall I put my shoes on the windowsill, like I did when I was a kid, in hopes there will be gifts in them in the morning?" teased Vida.

Grandma chuckled and gave Vida an extra big hug. The special time spent with family in Mexico went all too quickly. Everyone visited for as many days possible, and then it was time to catch a plane and fly home with happy memories.

☙

Claire's doctor's visit scheduled for the day after Christmas went well. As much as Claire secretly hoped the pregnancy tests were faulty, but she knew she was pregnant. By that time, with all her symptoms, to think otherwise was silly. Still, the way she had gotten pregnant wouldn't leave her. She tried to distract herself from those memories by thinking about her baby. *Her baby.* No matter how the pregnancy happened, she was determined to be the best mother she could. *This might be my only chance to have a baby now that Alan is dead.* It was another thought she kept coming back to, and it was morbid, but she couldn't help but feel it.

Alan had been gone less than a year, and grief was a slingshot, flinging her into one emotion and then another and another. All the articles she read online about the stages of grief were baloney. There was no chart you could follow to tell you how you would feel on any given day. Grief was just a terrible ride you had to strap yourself into and hang on until it stopped. *When will that be?* Claire wondered.

After a few more errands and some shopping, Claire would be ready to leave for Chloe's. The days after Christmas were filled with chipping away at her work projects, ensuring her laptop was tuned up for the trip and writing out instructions to Ellie and Vida, who planned to check on her apartment. A few friends from work had invited Claire to spend New Year's Eve with them, and even though Ellie had a date for New Year's Eve with her longtime boyfriend, Joe, she had invited Claire to join them. But a quiet night at home sounded best to Claire.

"Thanks, Ellie," Claire responded. "I think I will be happiest to stay home and finish up some last-minute prep before I leave." As the office would be closed for two weeks for the holidays, Claire and Ellie would say their goodbyes on New Year's Day. She and Vida had already hugged until "next time" before Vida took off to fly to her family's.

Saying goodbye to Ellie arrived sooner than Claire thought. Time was flying in so many ways but creeping along in others. When she was worried, nestled up in the corner of her couch, all Claire could feel was every minute ticking by, but when it came to saying ta-ta-for-now, she had no idea how the day had already arrived.

"I will miss you so much, Claire," Ellie said standing in Claire's hallway. "Nothing will be the same without you at the office." Ellie smiled at her wistfully and squeezed her hands. "I'm here if you need anything at all. Please, call me anytime. I just know your sister will take such good care of you. But in the middle of the night if ..."

Claire laughed and smoothed a tendril of hair off Ellie's cheek. "You're a silly goose! I'll call you. Of course I will, and I will miss you every day! But you call me, too."

Now Claire fought back tears, and Ellie scolded her. "Stop that, or we'll just be two puddles in this hallway!"

Claire sniffed. "Hopefully, I'll be back at the office after the baby is born. We'll have so much to catch up on. I'll be missing you too!" Claire said. "I just love your face, El! You've done so much for me."

"Friendship, duh," Ellie joked.

It was the perfect lighthearted note to end their goodbye on.

Chapter 11

Scotty took advantage of the time off from work and accepted an invitation to spend the holidays with Lucy and her family in Kokomo, Indiana. Lucy's parents had a sprawling seven-room house with plenty of room for Scotty to stay with them, in a separate bedroom of course. Most of his dark thoughts and headaches had taken a holiday, too. That happened a lot when he was with Lucy. Lucy's family had decorated a large tree and put several wrapped gifts under it. A Nativity set highlighted the mantle. Scotty wondered if any of the gifts were for him.

He couldn't remember much of Christmas when he was a kid. His memories were mostly of being scolded, plotting some mischief, or worse. When he had first met Lucy's three brothers—even all those years ago—Scotty knew they didn't like him. *Okay, buds, I don't much care for any of you either*, he'd thought, with a fake smile on his face. And it was the same now. Time hadn't healed anything.

He tried to plan time away from the house to take a drive with Lucy or get out somewhere, anywhere. But that meant using more gas for the car—money he didn't have. When they were alone, Lucy tightened the pressure valve when she drilled him on picking a wedding date.

"Scotty, I know you love me, and I love you, but do you have any idea when we will be able to be married?" They were sitting in the car at a stoplight, snowflakes melting against the windows. Shadows of rivulets moving on her cheeks. She was trying to be so endearing and cute, the way she clasped her hands and nuzzled his shoulder.

"Lucy, sweetheart, I just need to put a little more money away before we can be married, so we can have a nice apartment in a safe neighborhood." Scott turned to peer into her gray eyes, and his stomach clenched like it was trying to juggle rocks. All he did was disappoint her. He couldn't stand seeing her little lips flip into a frown.

Lucy asked a little more quietly this time—and dammit, was that a tear in her eye? "When will that be? How much longer am I supposed to wait? Do you really love me, or are you stringing me along?"

The rocks in Scotty's stomach grew hot. Like lava. Then his whole body was blazing hot, and it was the queerest sensation when he looked at her—her slender white neck above her pleading face. He wanted to smash it in with his fists. Instead, he huffed with barely concealed control, "Don't give me an ultimatum, Lucy. Is that a nice thing to do? I'm trying as hard as I can but this all takes money. Feel free to kick in some cash yourself. Aren't you a modern woman?"

Lucy's eyes turned to stormy seas. She raised her eyebrows, her words cutting, "I am tired of this arrangement. And when are you going to give me an engagement ring?" The more she spoke, the more her words caught fire. She rattled off her thoughts so fast. "NOW you want me to chip in for my own wedding? What kind of bride does that? Not this one!" She sighed heavily and was silent for a few minutes, as Scotty fought to breathe evenly, before oozing, "Scotty, baby, let's not fight. I'm just trying to move us forward. I want us to be together. I know you don't want to spend the rest of your life sleeping in the guest room."

Scotty shrugged, cooling a little. "I miss you in there."

Lucy smiled again. How was it that every time she did, his heart melted, and his stomach flopped around but not in the bad, hot way? She made his anger and urges disappear.

"Of course you do." Lucy was tender. "So how about we plan a spring wedding? Will you have enough money saved by then? I bet you will, sweetie!"

Small wrinkles surfaced on Scotty's forehead as he wrestled with the panic rising in his throat. He ordered himself to calm down as his knuckles turned white on the steering wheel. "I will make it happen, somehow, Lucy. You know how much I love you."

That seemed to do the trick. Lucy sat back in her seat and fiddled with her silk scarf. *Why does she need such expensive things?* Scotty thought. He had figured she would give up on needing so much, but the more time they spent together, the worse it got.

What he had told Lucy was to placate her. He knew full well that his current bank account couldn't support her dreams. That wasn't changing anytime soon. He had to think up another way to get the money but had no idea how.

A few days later, with the holidays over, and Lucy dropped off with a passionate goodbye, Scotty drove home. As sleet slashed at the windows, he contemplated how to get his hands on a lot of loot. Lucy did deserve a ring. When he imagined the kind of ring she wanted, his temperature went up. Why couldn't she just be happy with what he could provide her? It wasn't much, but wasn't love supposed to mean more than money?

Scotty cared about Lucy. He felt calm when he was with her. As much as he was frustrated at her pushing, he knew he had to come up with a solution. Lucy was his ticket out of his black thoughts. When he thought of her, he could see them growing old together. He could see living differently—with less fear that he would slip and end up in the slammer.

Alone, with the heat streaming on him and slush sliding down the window, life was hard. His moods were hard. Finding the solution to shut Lucy up was hard. It was all so damned hard!

He was tempted to speed up the timeline by doing something drastic like he had done when he was young. And there, in the car, he wrestled with himself, driving and sliding along, his voice barely above a whisper. "I can't do anything too risky or be caught doing something illegal. I won't relive that horrible school—the naughty place. Why can't some people just shut up? They need to be shut up."

Scotty gritted his teeth and tried to push away the intrusive thoughts. He still wanted to hurt people and animals. The naughty place had explained that it was wrong, that they could help him, but he'd only pretended to get better. The voices in his head did not go away. Sometimes, they were louder than before. Then came the day that he answered the voices, the people who were as real to him as if he was standing beside them jabbering about the weather. They warned him, but he couldn't get their full message. It only made him listen harder. Maybe some lucky day, he would hear every thought in their lightless hearts.

The feeling was dark, hot, like the hot rocks in his gut. They wanted him to act out on their behalf. By this point, he had gotten quite practiced at pretending he was cured. It wasn't that hard if you set your mind to it, just a study in human behavior to somewhat fit in. To get a job with regular people, to make certain impressionable girls date you, and *I guess fall in love with you?* Scotty's mouth curled at the thought of Lucy. Somehow, in a way that the naughty place had assured him would never happen, he loved her back.

"I'm that good," he told the whipping windshield wipers. Now it was pretty easy to blend in—unless people got too close. That never had a good ending. So far faking it till he was making it had been enough to keep him out of any more mental health facilities. He knew if he stepped over the line, if he hurt someone and got caught, it would be prison.

As Scotty drove home to his aunt's house, the same question tormented him. "What is the answer to getting enough money for the wedding, for Lucy, for everything?" Not knowing what to do, how to make Lucy stop with her incessant questions, and please everyone around him, kept him up at night. He roamed the house when his dear auntie was asleep, sometimes finding himself outside her door, staring through it as if he could peer inside to her sleeping form. Then he would shake his head hard to keep himself from opening the door and giving in to his demons.

The memories of his love and hate of her swirled in his head like the most terrifying nightmare painted by the most unholy thoughts a person could conjure.

He turned down the street to his aunt's house, the streetlights dim in the falling snow. He parked on the driveway. "Never in the garage, Scott. That's where I hide my keepsakes." So he had to park in the snowy wasteland like a reject. By the time he got to the front door, his hair was plastered to his head. Water ran down his face.

The first thing Florence said to him before he was inside the door, was, "Scott, thank heavens you're home! The most dreadful thing has happened. A mouse got caught in that trap in the laundry room. You have to get rid of it right now. I haven't slept since I discovered it."

Geez, thought Scotty, *what a shitty welcome*. But aloud he muttered, "No problem, I'll take care of it ASAP."

After he dispatched of the little vermin, he ate a microwave dinner and went to bed. That night he slept for the first time in weeks.

The next day, the office was open again. Scotty arrived extra early, eager for the distraction of not dealing with Lucy's pressure and his aunt's obvious disinterest. Most of the staff arrived early, too. Before long, the office was abuzz with people laughing and telling stories of how wonderful their holidays had been. Scotty put his headphones on and hunkered down in his cubicle to drown out the noise.

Vida was one of the last to arrive. Her plane hadn't landed until late last night. She felt tired and a little sad at leaving her grandma. She was getting on in years, and every time Vida left her, she couldn't help but think it might be the last time. Vida blinked hard a couple of times to chase away the tears that threatened and scolded herself to get her head on straight and focus on work. She opened the side drawer to put her purse away, then let out a shriek loud enough to be heard up and down all of Michigan Avenue.

"There's a dead mouse inside my desk drawer!" she shrieked as she jumped up and away from her desk. Several people, including Ellie and Scotty, rushed over. "What's the matter, V?" Ellie asked, grabbing Vida's shoulders. Vida took a deep breath and gave her a quavery smile. "I was so scared! Goodness! My heart's pounding!" She laughed uneasily and Ellie let out a huge breath and lightly smacked Vida on her arm. "God, woman! I thought you were dying!" Now they were laughing a little as Scotty budged into their conversation.

"No need to get so upset, Vida. I'll take care of this little fella for you." Scotty smirked as he walked over to the desk drawer. He looked up at Vida and Ellie with an amused expression. "I wonder how he managed to get in there?"

"Beat it," Vida said as she marched over to her desk and shooed him away. "That's why we have a maintenance department, you weirdo!"

At the mention of "weirdo," Scotty's bemused expression evaporated from his face, replaced by red cheeks and a brittle smile.

One of the men removed the drawer and took it outside to clean it. Even though she had tried to laugh it off, Vida was still unnerved. No one could figure out how the mouse had gotten in the drawer, but Vida had some suspicions. *Why am I suspecting Scotty? Nah, he's just odd.*

She replayed their night together at Tortoise when she lied about her goings-on with Bryce. *He believed me—didn't he?* Even if he didn't, she couldn't imagine a sane person reacting in that matter. Maybe that was the problem. Maybe Scotty wasn't as normal as he tried to put out. That was it for Vida. She might as well have gone home for all her lack of concentration on her waiting projects. As Vida attempted to make her department's budget make sense, she couldn't stop thinking about evening the score: *Could I trick him into spilling the beans?*

☙

Claire finally called Brian, her fingers trembling as she punched in his number. She took a big breath and waited for him to answer the phone.

"Brian, hi!" she practically yelled at his "hello."

Brian laughed, and Claire tried to calm down. "I'm so sorry," she laughed. "I guess I'm easily startled these days."

Now Brian's voice was all concern. "Are you okay?"

"It's nothing like that," Claire lied. "I just wanted to let you know I'm going out of town to take care of my sister. She's having major back surgery and will be out of commission for quite some time. Mr. Andrews, my boss, is being so great about it. I'm going to be working remotely—when I'm not babysitting my niece and nephew."

"I'm so sorry to hear about your sister." Brian's voice was deep and soothing. "If it weren't for her surgery, sounds like it might be a pretty awesome time."

"I think it will be anyway. Chloe and I are very close. She's been like a mother to me. And I can't get enough of those kids!"

Claire didn't want to hang up the phone, and before they knew it, forty-five minutes had passed. Brian shared all about his holiday but let her know that "This Christmas wasn't as bright as it usually is. Alan was severely missed. So were you." His voice dropped an octave.

At that, Claire's heart sped up again. "I miss you, too," she managed to get out. "But," she replied smartly, remembering to pull it together—*why was Brian making her feel so nervous?*—"I promise I'll call you when I get home. We can get together then."

"Okay, sunshine." There was a clear smile in Brian's voice. It warmed Claire like she was sitting on her balcony on a summer day. "I hope Chloe's surgery goes well and that you don't go crazy with those kiddos!"

Claire chuckled. "We'll see …"

"She's lucky to have you," Brian said. "I can't wait to see you when you return."

After hanging up, Claire felt terrible about lying to Brian, but the fewer people who knew about the pregnancy the better. Brian included—until she could let him in on it. *But why do you care? She chastised herself. That's Alan's brother! What are you thinking? And you're PREGNANT!* "Ugh!" She hit the arm of the sofa. "Knock it off and get back to getting on the road!"

Claire eased herself off the couch, a strange sadness about leaving her apartment hovering over her. This was the closing of a chapter. When she returned home from Chloe's, she would be a mother and never alone again. It was exhilarating and terrifying all at once. Some moments almost brought her to her knees, she was so overwhelmed, and some made her feel like she was soaring. All she could do was take each day at a time, a minute at a time if she had to. Then there was missing Alan so deeply that her body actually hurt. And now, what was going on with Brian? *Isn't this wrong?* Thinking about him brought a smile to her tired face as she made her way to the rear of the apartment.

She walked into the second bedroom and surveyed it, deciding that the items she'd bought and had delivered were all in place for the baby. She had arranged ahead of time to have the delivery people put the crib together, as well as handle any other tough jobs like baby-proofing the apartment. Logistically, she had all the necessary things for the baby. "I hope I didn't forget anything," she worried as she looked around the room once more. It didn't look like a well-loved and lived-in nursery yet. Any decorating could wait until she arrived home with her baby—whoever he or she was. That is, if she decided to decorate at all. How long she could live in a downtown apartment with a growing baby had to be considered. Her head was spinning with all the changes in her life. They piled on top of her until she felt she was suffocating.

Claire felt for the wall behind her, relieved to find it was still there as she slid down it to sit on the floor. "I hope to God I can handle all this." She put her face in her hands and cried a little. After a couple of minutes, she picked herself up and wiped her eyes. Lingering in the doorway, she said aloud, "Maybe being with Chloe and taking her advice about babies will calm my nerves. She'll help me find some peace."

Claire softly closed the nursery door and padded into her bedroom across the hall. She checked her bags for the umpteenth time. *Comfy clothes for around the house, toiletries, and a couple of nice outfits in case we go out to dinner.* She tried to limit what she was bringing to two large suitcases, not wanting to scare Chloe and Lou into thinking she was moving in permanently. *I'd better not bring too much. They will think I am here to stay!* She whispered aloud to no one, "What will they think when I tell them I am pregnant? I suppose I should tell them the entire story. This truly is a nightmare, only dammit, it's REAL!!"

All at once, it was almost too much again. But eventually, she finally set foot out of her house and locked the door behind her. She had already given extra keys to Ellie and Vida and notified the management company they would be coming and going to keep an eye on the place.

The drive to Chloe's was uneventful with a little light snow that didn't stick. "All good, so far," Claire decided as she put some soft rock on the radio. Soon, she was singing along to some of her favorites and nearing Chloe's charming little town. Horses dotted vast pastures and stomped their feet at her passing. The sun climbed high in the sky, and the snow cleared up. The blue stretched above her was a sparkling jewel, and she tried to make her spirits match it.

Chloe's family greeted her with warm hugs. Melissa and Michael squealed with delight that the aunt they adored was going to stay with them to hopefully play lots of games and read lots and lots of books. Claire tickled and hugged them, and they helped her unpack as they told her all about the best hiding spots in the house—because "For sure, we *are* playing hide and seek, Auntie!"

Claire couldn't argue with Melissa, who had an adorable slight lisp, and Michael bursting about the new indoor swim place. "It's gots light and everything. You can go at *night!*" Michael was beside himself until he picked up Claire's nightgown. "Gross!" he yelled and skipped out of the room. Claire and Melissa shared a look and laughed. "Boys, am I right, Auntie?" Then she, too, darted off, leaving Claire to finish unpacking by herself in between laughter as she lost herself in the pure joy and silliness of the two kids.

Chloe and Lou had put so much thought into making her feel at home. As Claire looked around, she thought, *I can put my computer on that desk in front of the windows and watch the seasons changing as I work.* A twin bed anchored one wall, and a small, fluffy throw rug was under her feet. Claire took off her shoes and wiggled her toes in it. *Leave it to Chloe to make me never want to leave.*

Dinner was relaxed and delicious. Chloe had always been the best cook. She was a foodie ahead of her time, researching recipes and ingredients, making every dish Claire could imagine exquisite. Melissa and Michael didn't even complain about the meal. Sitting around the table with her family made Claire feel better. After dinner, Chloe put the kids to bed, and when she came back downstairs, Claire realized she had to tell Chloe and Lou the entire hideous story. Her voice shook the whole time, and she dabbed at her eyes with her napkin, finishing by placing her hands on her belly and issuing a weak smile. "And now, we're here," she said, glancing downward.

Both Chloe and Lou were full of concern. "Are you sure you're okay?" Chloe asked, her brows knitted in the middle of her forehead. She walked around the table and hugged Claire, who gratefully buried her head in Chloe's shoulder, and cried a bit more. Chloe was warm and soothing like she'd always been, her hair smelling of wildflowers.

Lou had a different reply. "That bastard deserved to die," he hollered as Chloe shushed him. "You'll wake the kids!"

Claire lifted her head from Chloe's shoulder. "No, what he did was despicable, but he didn't deserve to die. I am the one responsible. How can I ever forgive myself?"

Chloe squeezed Claire a little tighter but didn't answer. Claire supposed there was no answer anyway. "Let's get you to bed, sweetie," Chloe soothed. "You must be exhausted."

At the doorway of Claire's room, Chloe said, "We can make an appointment with my obstetrician whenever you are ready. I'll go with you, of course. I mean, if you want me to. The kids will be back in school after the Christmas break."

"I'd love for you to come along." Claire smiled and realized how tired she was. The day's drive and bouncing back and forth between all her feelings had positively wiped her out. She yawned and said, "Yes, let's do that, I'm anxious to get that appointment set up and meet the doctor."

After the sisters said their goodnights, Claire climbed into the comfy bed. She felt at peace and very grateful. *If I could just work remotely all the time* were the last words on her mind before she fell into a deep, dreamless sleep.

The next day, Claire lucked out again. Chloe's OBGYN had an opening in a couple of hours due to a cancellation. The plan was to go and squeeze in lunch afterward. Even though Claire's life had blown up, she was truly enjoying her sister's company. Like always, when she was with Chloe, she never wanted their time to end.

Chapter 12

With money worries hanging over him, Scotty anguished over what to do. These thoughts pestered at him as he tried to go about his daily life, a feat he was finding more and more difficult the more pressure that was laid on him.

Should I break into a jewelry store? he wondered one day, waiting for his coffee. *I could easily grab a gorgeous diamond ring for Lucy. Then I could bring the jewelry to a fence, and they would take it off my hands and hand over the money.*

"Hey, buddy," the barista said, "not sure what you're mumbling about, but the total is $8.59 without tip."

Scotty blinked a few times, then said peevishly, "Why would I give you a tip? You're not a waiter."

"No, sir, I'm not." The barista leveled him with a glare. He pointed at the end of the counter. "You can get your drink in that line."

Scotty wandered away to the other end of the room, still brainstorming on possible scenarios to get him out of his financial mess.

"How would I approach a bank teller? I'd have to have a gun. Where do I buy a gun?"

"Scott?" Another barista yelled out, popping Scotty's malicious bubble. "Right here!" He charged up to the bar, a finger in the air as if punctuating the point. Drink in hand, and the eyes of patrons on his back amidst a few nervous giggles, he slunk out the door.

Without any answers Scotty's misery escalated. His head throbbed as he sat in the car and sipped his drink. The pain was alarmingly strong. "What am I going to do?" he said. Whatever he would do, it was becoming clear that he had to do something, "or my head just might explode."

☙

Vida was still obsessing over the idea that Scotty was the culprit who'd put the dead mouse in her desk drawer and slashed her tires. She just couldn't come up with a plausible reason why, even if he hadn't believed her at the restaurant. Then one day, in between bites of Cobb salad at her desk, she slammed her fork down suddenly convinced she really hadn't put one over on him. *He knows it's Claire's compact and that I LIED. I lied to a psychopath!*

I suppose I should tell Claire, not that Claire needs any more bad news.

She had no idea that, close by, Scotty was fighting his own dilemmas.

He entertained so many possibilities in his sick mind of how to get some money. Finally, it dawned on him and his jumbled thoughts cleared from his mind, Scotty turned into the shining example of the perfect employee for the rest of the day.

That night at dinner with Florence, Scotty asked, "Auntie, why don't you ever wear any jewelry? I bet you have some beautiful pieces."

Florence wadded her old face into a smile and squinted into his face. "I have my share of nice jewelry, Scotty. But I haven't worn any of it in years." She seemed a little sad as she picked at her mashed potatoes.

Scotty said brightly, "How about after dinner you show me all your lovely jewelry. You can recall all the happy days when you wore it," gushed Scotty. "I would love to see it."

Florence set her fork down and grinned at him. "All right," she declared. "It will be fun to look at all of it again, and it's been ages since I've done that." She gave him a look that would've melted any other nephew, but it made Scotty's skin crawl. "How very sweet of you to ask. You have such great ideas."

They finished dinner, and Florence scooted to the bedroom to retrieve her jewelry box. Scotty remained seated at the table. Soon Aunt Florence stepped through the doorway. She leaned on her cane with one hand, and in the other, cradled a large wooden box. Scotty took the box from her and set it on the table. Aunt Florence eased down into the seat beside him.

"Now, what shall I show you first?" Florence croaked in her dusty voice. She sifted through the jewelry with her gnarled fingers, then plucked up a few pieces. "See here, I have a precious pearl necklace with earrings to match." She smiled, her lips displaying gleaming overly white dentures. Her eyes were alight as she lost herself in memories. "I have this old brooch set with diamonds and rubies. But, you know, Scotty, I hardly ever wore it. Your Uncle Arthur gave it to me one anniversary when we were overlooking the French Riviera. Oh yes, I was on a cloud that day!" Scotty smiled and nodded in all the right places as he controlled himself from drumming his fingers on the table in impatience. *Get to it, you old woman* screamed his mind. "Yes, yes, stunning indeed." He made sure to speak slowly and as if he simply couldn't wait to hear more. "What other treasures do you have in that box?" He hoped his voice belied his lack of excitement.

By then Florence was deep down memory lane. "And here is my engagement ring. Take a look at that gorgeous center diamond, would you? My gracious, I remember when Arthur asked me to marry him." She smiled as she clutched the ring between her fingers. "He surprised me with this ring. Did you know that? I had no idea he was going to propose. So many times, he'd fooled me, and honestly, I'd just set the notion off to the side …" Scotty forced a slight smile and nod. "I know that, Auntie. He was quite the smooth talker."

"You're missing the point, dear," Aunt Florence tut-tutted. "He wasn't that at all. Just the most sincere man I've ever—"

"My mistake," Scotty spoke quickly.

Florence was back in her own world. "So many more lovely pieces. I had forgotten how many." She replaced her jewelry into the box and shut the box with a clunk. Then folding her hands and with a peaceful aura about her, she turned to Scott, "That was pleasant. Thank you, Scott, for suggesting I bring the jewelry box out and recall so many happy memories."

"Where do you keep that jewelry box with all those treasures? Aren't you worried that maybe you should store them in a safer place?"

"I am here alone most of the time. In fact, you are the only one besides me who is ever here. I don't have visitors anymore. All my friends have passed on." She spoke this last part in a low tone before popping back into the present.

"If you must know, I keep the box in the bottom drawer of my bureau." She stared at him hard for a second, then lifted her ample form from the table, murmuring under her breath, "Not that it's any of your business," then louder, "I'll put it back where it belongs." She picked the box back up and grabbed her cane from where it rested against the table.

Scotty flushed deep red at her words, then *accidentally* positioned his foot at the base of the cane, giving a small shove, then *voilà!*

The cane slipped, and Florence went down with a loud thud. She whimpered for second before her voice strengthened to a yell and tears stuck in her wrinkled face. "Scott! I heard a crack! I think I broke something. Oh, the pain is terrible! Please get help!"

Scotty leaped up from the table and raced to the phone on the wall. He dialed 911. As the paramedics were strapping her onto the gurney, Scotty paced around, asking over and over again, "How could this have happened?" Once Florence was loaded into the ambulance and on the way to the hospital, Scotty followed behind in his car. It was hard to keep his mind on the mission of acting as normally as possible as he drove. But he had to put out the vibe that nothing was wrong. Once Florence was checked in and on her way to X-ray, Scotty ducked out, practically salivating, envisioning the *jewelry*. He drove home as fast as he could, pushing from his mind how Florence would react when she realized he'd left her at the hospital.

When he stepped in the door, the phone rang, startling him. Florence didn't have caller ID or anything like that, so he had no idea who was calling, and besides, he had other plans. The caller hung up, but then the phone rang again and again and again ... Still, he never picked it up. But he didn't move an inch to do what he'd returned to do until that blasted phone was silent.

☙

Claire's doctor's appointment went well. She immediately liked Dr. Martha Blakely, a young obstetrician with a large practice. She was a month and a half along by then. "Everything looks great," Dr. Blakely said with a smile. She turned to wash her hands in the sink, then directed Claire to make her upcoming appointments at the scheduling desk. Claire left the office feeling confident that all would work out well.

After the appointment, Claire and Chloe had plenty of time for a bowl of chili and hot coffee at the local cafe. When they returned home, Claire headed upstairs for a short nap before she logged in for the day to work. *I am so grateful and relieved, thanks to my wonderful sister*, she thought, as she drifted off.

☙

Finally, Florence's phone stopped ringing, easing the pain in Scotty's head. He was so wracked with agony, that he didn't hear the front door open and Florence walking in. Even the distinctive thump of her cane on the floor couldn't shake him from his reverie. Florence gasped when she saw Scotty with her jewelry spread out on the dining room table. "What are you doing?" she demanded.

As Scotty looked her over, she seemed just the same, like the fall hadn't done a damn thing to the old bird. His heart beat fast as he peered into her face. *How could she be home already?*

"I, uh, I was just admiring all your lovely pieces again, Aunt Florence."

Florence stared open-mouthed at him for a minute before her eyes hardened. "Do you think I'm a nitwit? How dare you go through my things without my permission!"

"Don't you dare scold me, you old bat!" Scotty leaned forward on the table, leering at her. "I am sick of you calling all the shots around here and charging me rent and parking—when I can't even use your godforsaken garage. You don't need the money. You just do it to spite me. I hate you, do you hear me?"

In a fury, Scotty ripped away Florence's cane from her grasp. She stumbled before catching herself on a chair. Scotty raised the cane and brought it down as hard as he could on her frail body. Florence screamed, "Scotty, STOP! Are you crazy? You are hurting me. STOP IT NOW!"

"You are nothing more than a selfish old bag!" Scotty laughed then cried, the cane railing up and down as Florence fell to the floor and writhed around.

He raged on. "Here you go bitch! Here's your cane. Cry all you want!" He dropped the cane next to her bloody body, then ran out of the house, cackling a weird little laugh as he took off into the night.

Scotty ran for a couple of blocks, but he had no idea what he was doing anymore. He didn't know where to go and couldn't even think. Finally, he spotted a house with a small portico jutting out from the backyard.

He crawled over to the portico, and sat inside trembling, his arms locked around his knees. *What can I do next?* Everything leading up to this moment was gone. Suddenly, Scotty couldn't understand how he was plunked down in the dirt under a house. All he knew was to stay put. A feeling told him to be still for a while, that he would know when it was time to leave. Scotty listened to the feeling. He would hide in the dirt as long as he needed to.

As soon as Florence could muster enough strength, she made her way to the telephone and called the police. Her voice was faint as she rasped out the details of her nephew almost beating her to death. "I don't know where he went!" she said in a queer breathless whisper. "Please, just catch him! He'll kill me! He'll kill me," she sobbed.

Chapter 13

The weeks and months were rolling along for Claire. She had grown out of her regular size and now wore the bigger tops and the stretchy pants she'd packed for her stay at Chloe's.

The company's workload was heavy, but Claire didn't mind. She was grateful she could do the job successfully while staying with her sister and her family. As she worked every day in her room overlooking Chloe's storybook yard with all the different species of flowers and trees, it was inevitable that signs of spring slowly unfolded. The snow was long gone by then, and a few tiny green buds were visible if you looked carefully.

In her second trimester, Claire felt well and reinvigorated. That was a blessing as both Melissa and Michael tried to enlist her in any and all of their games. Spending all the extra time with her niece and nephew was a plus. She adored them, and it was obvious that the feeling was mutual.

She still saw Dr. Blakely once a month, but that would change as she neared her due date. Dr. Blakely assured her everything was fine and going along as beautifully as she could imagine.

If she only knew the truth. It was a thought Claire often had, even as she accompanied Chloe on her grocery shopping. Kindly strangers smiled warmly at her in the little town, and Claire felt a little ashamed of the secret she held back. She gamely lied when confronted with a question about her pregnancy by an innocent-stranger "Yes, my husband and I are so excited about our new baby," Claire would reply, coaxing a smile onto her face. Then she would toddle along, and her heart would drop. Chloe would usually take her hand and give it a squeeze.

There were no words to describe the war waging inside her. She wished so fervently that the baby could be Alan's. That would make everything all right, but so would Alan being *alive*. No matter how hard she tried, she couldn't change the past. She couldn't take away the weight that pressed down on her, on top of the pregnancy. And she wondered if it would haunt her for the rest of her life.

Once, as she and Chloe were standing at the kitchen counter peeling carrots for the dinner salad, Chloe brought up adoption.

"Don't be mad at me, okay? But maybe adoption would be easier—considering the way you conceived?" Chloe smiled gently, and Claire couldn't help it, she smiled back—but just a little.

"I could never be mad at you, and I've already considered it. But there's something about finding the only good in something so horrible that could've ruined my life forever. It makes me feel stronger—if that makes any sense."

Chloe picked up the peeler and a carrot. She resumed peeling. "It makes perfect sense. I mean, I can understand because you and I think alike. But it has to be so hard to want to feel the joy and share it all with a husband or even a boyfriend. I'm so mad at Bryce!"

Claire smiled again, but a tear dropped down her cheek and made a wet splotch on her shirt. "He was sick, Clo. We have to remember that. His sickness made him do things. And in all of that, I was given a beautiful baby—for whatever reason. But I just have to cling to the feeling this child is going to change me. I'm going to change them, or him, her, whatever, too."

Claire wiped her eyes on a kitchen towel as Chloe made the fragrant orange pile in front of them grow larger. Claire scooped up the peelings and put them in a bowl. "I wouldn't be a good sister unless I brought it up. You know that, right?"

"Please stop worrying you're going to say the wrong thing!" Claire said almost sharply. Then she softened and said, "I just don't want you to tiptoe around me. I'm not frail."

Chloe grabbed another carrot and peeled away. A few minutes passed with the sisters working in silence. Then Chloe blurted out, "So you're not curious about the gender of the baby at all?"

"Not really," Claire said and patted her stomach. "I'm going to get who I'm supposed to, and they're going to get me. Maybe they even chose me?"

Chloe raised her eyebrows as Claire continued, "But for some reason, I do think I'm having a boy, a little Alan. Or maybe it's wishful thinking?"

"Maybe you're psychic?" Chloe joked.

"Who knows," Claire said and grabbed the mayonnaise out of the fridge. She set it on the counter and worked on untwisting the lid. "But I will NOT name him Alan. Maybe Alan for a middle name?"

"That sounds nice," Chloe affirmed and then asked, her eyes suddenly large as she took in the pile of peelings, "Wait, how many carrots do we need anyway?"

Claire eyed the mound in the bowl and laughed hard. "I was going to ask the same thing. I think ... we went overboard!"

They both laughed themselves into fits as they finished cooking dinner together, and if you had asked Claire for her definition of a perfect day, this would have been it. But with *Alan*, she reminded herself. *Or Brian?*

⁂

Ellie and Vida were still working at the marketing firm as Claire worked remotely at her sister's. Every day felt mostly the same, with one exception: Scotty was no longer employed there. There was no official announcement or anything by their leadership team, but tongues wagged that he was in a "special" hospital. *No release date at this time* went the rumor mill.

Strange, thought Vida, *I wonder what that oddball has done now?* In a sense, she didn't care much. He was off her back. There were no more flat tires or dead animals in her drawers. That was good enough for her. *RIP, moron*, she thought as she tackled her work with new energy. When she spoke to Ellie at lunch that day, she had no insight into what had happened, either. It seemed the bizarre case of "Who the hell is Scotty Hawkins?" was closed.

Then Ellie suggested, around a mouthful of salmon, "Vida, would you like to take a road trip and visit Claire?"

Vida clapped her hands and bounced up and down in the booth. "Oh yes! That is an excellent idea. When would you like to go? It has to be on a weekend and at a time that works for Claire, but I am wide open."

The girls called Claire together right that second, and her enthusiasm spilled out of the phone. "I would absolutely love that! How about next weekend?"

After more chit-chat and discussion of the news of Scotty, the three hung up, eager to get back together. With Claire gone, the trio was incomplete. Soon, they would be reunited.

Midday the following Saturday, Ellie's car crunched over the gravel leading up to Chloe and Lou's house. After introductions to everyone, to the delight of a squealing Michael and Melissa, Claire showed the gals her homey bedroom.

The girls prattled on about how perfect Claire's desk was with a view into the flower gardens and birds flitting about from branch to branch.

"I have been so comfortable living here. Chloe and Lou have made me feel so welcome. They have been just wonderful," Claire said.

"That makes both of us happy, Claire. Good for you," Vida replied. "We've been a little worried, and now we know that's just silly. You're obviously set up and adored! Yay!" She clapped.

"I'm so happy for you, too, Claire!" Ellie enthused. She flounced down on Claire's bed. "Now, we have to squeeze as much fun as we can into our short visit. Where to first?"

"Let's check out the bed and breakfast I reserved for you," Claire said. "I hope you'll like it. It's the old Vrooman Mansion, built in 1869. Such a masterpiece! Stained glass windows, leather furniture, down comforters, and comfy beds. You will love it and never want to leave."

"So that's your master plan?" Ellie teased.

"Maybe," Claire teased back. "Anyway, it's very comfortable. But it's a good thing you aren't wearing heels. The stair treads and risers are a lot smaller than we're used to. People were smaller in those days."

"You sound like a tour guide!" Vida chided. "Are they paying you for every guest you book?"

"I'm just excited you're here," Claire chuckled. "I've been waiting forever for you two to get your heinies down here! But back to the mansion. It's got great food, and breakfast is included."

"Does that conclude the tour?" Ellie asked. "And here we didn't even leave your bedroom!"

They all had a good laugh, and after bidding goodbye and assuring Michael and Melissa she would indeed be back, the three trooped off to the mansion to check in.

Once Ellie and Vida had dropped off their bags, they headed for brunch. Again, Claire chose a small old-fashioned, family-owned restaurant that served home cookin'.

Predictably, there was lots of catch-up time. Their conversation was punctuated with "Did you know this?" "Did I tell you that? So many laughs mixed in with their happy and content feelings.

Window shopping followed brunch, and then they all returned to their rooms for a little rest before dinner that night.

Chloe insisted on hosting a "home-loved meal." "It's a promotion over 'homemade,'" she told everyone. They all gathered around the table as Chloe served a decadent four-course dinner complete with shrimp appetizers.

Lou remarked how joyful everyone seemed to be now that they were together again. And Michael and Melissa had to get their two cents in, although, through gentle redirects, Lou made sure their input was kept to a minimum.

Vida patted her belly and smiled, "That was dee-licious! Thank you, I am beyond stuffed."

"Talk about an unforgettable home-loved meal," Ellie commented. "I haven't had anything that good in ages. So sweet of you to cook for us."

After a little more catching up—it seemed like they couldn't squeeze enough words into their day—it was time to turn in for the night. All three would gather again for breakfast in the morning then Ellie and Vida would start the drive home. Before the girls left for the night, they convinced Chloe to join them to make their trio a quartet. She graciously accepted.

Bright and early, Claire soon learned the real reason behind their breakfast. Ellie and Vida presented Claire with a car seat to bring the baby home from the hospital.

Claire was beyond touched at their thoughtfulness and generosity. "I really haven't bought much for the baby. Chloe is lending me a bassinet she had in the attic. I got some diapers and bottles, and I don't plan to nurse, so I did buy formula." She waved her hands in the air. "Ahhh! I feel crazy! There's so much to do! I haven't decided on any names, but maybe Richard James?"

Vida and Ellie knew how conflicted Claire's feelings were. They exchanged glances with Chloe and could tell she felt the same.

In her ever-constant good-natured sarcasm, Vida piped up: "Richard James? No. Are you giving birth to a king?"

Claire feigned mock surprise and shock, setting the women off into fresh laughter again. She could tell her sister and friends were doing their damnedest to keep her laughing, not crying.

And she appreciated that, but the reality always came back—as realities and consequences tend to do.

Despite how she had conceived, a mother's feelings when bringing a baby into the world were inevitable. Her baby was already loved beyond measure, surrounded by all the aunties who would spoil him or her forever. Mostly, Claire was getting excited about meeting her child, but there was always that darker layer. Her world had forever changed because of one man's lust for control. Now she had to live with the consequences—bad and amazing. At the very back of her mind, she wondered whose genes this child would get. She hoped it inherited nothing from its father.

After refills of coffee—decaf for Claire—the women sadly realized it was time to say goodbye. The quartet shared big warm hugs and wishes for a safe trip home. Claire was so sad to see her cherished friends leave. She stood and threw kisses between tears as Vida and Ellie rolled out of the parking lot to make the long trip home. Chloe tried her best to cheer her up as they drove back to the house, but Claire wasn't in the mood to talk much and finally turned her head to stare out the window.

Chapter 14

Scotty's days in the "special" hospital were full of highs and lows. Mostly lows. His new medication didn't quell the horrible, grisly thoughts that filled his mind. X-rays showed not a tumor but a small mass. They had done a quick biopsy and determined it wasn't malignant. If they removed the mass, the doctors said he would be rid of his thoughts of harming people. He would be cured of the turmoil always brewing in his brain. Scotty had no idea what that would even feel like. He had been the way he was for so long. At the farthest reaches of his memory lingered a vision of a youngster who enjoyed life, loved being outside, and even played little league. That little boy, who Scotty knew was him but felt like another person in another life, was so out of touch. Scotty listened without saying a word as the doctor explained everything going on in his prefrontal lobe, but he couldn't take in the information. *Who will I be now?* was all he could think.

Scotty hated who he was even as he hated other people. All his life, he had prayed—if that's what you could call it—to be normal like the rest of the world. He could see other people around him with spouses and kids, and that was an impossibility—he even had his doubts about Lucy now. The surgery might give him a chance to have a boring ol' life with Lucy. Hopefully, that would make her stick around. It sounded like a dream he was afraid to believe. *Is all this crap not my fault?* He didn't know how to feel about that. And he had no idea if Lucy would even love the new him. She had only been to see him once in the hospital. It was a very awkward visit, with Lucy making a lame excuse to leave earlier than she'd planned. "I really do have to get back to my meal prep for the week, or I won't have any lunch to eat. Hang in there," she said before leaning over and hugging him briefly. Scotty tried to pull her to him for a kiss, but she turned her head and ducked out of his embrace. Then she darted to the door, waving as she disappeared around the corner.

꽃

Brian kept thinking about Claire and wondering how she was doing. He was the only one who had a true inkling of the extent of her pain at losing Alan. And even though they'd had their separate relationships, the pain was crushing. Sometimes, that was all you needed to feel close to another person—a glimpse into a fraction of their pain. He wondered if that was why he couldn't get her off his mind lately.

One day, the pain of not seeing her overcame him, and as much as that surprised, thrilled, and alarmed him, Brian didn't mind it, and he sure didn't know that Claire felt the same guilty-thrilled way. Finally, his urges to see her took over, and before he knew it, he found himself standing at the reception desk of Claire's marketing firm.

The receptionist, a young lady with shiny black bangs, told Brian in a chipper voice when he asked about Claire, "Nope! Claire's not in this office anymore!" Brian stood there dressed as he always was in his usual black turtleneck shirt and slim black pants, his signature pop of color, loud print socks. He had dozens of pairs, and when people got a glimpse of his ankles when his pants rose as he sat down, they provoked fun questions and observations. Today's socks had violins. "I know that. Sorry if I wasn't clear. I'm trying to get an address to send her something."

"You know I can't share that with you," the receptionist's eyes blazed into his.

"No, no, it's nothing like that," Brian started sweating a little. "I mean, you can send her flowers—on me, of course. I really don't need her address."

"You know what," Ms. Trendy said, "I don't know what to do with you. One minute, please."

"Everett!" Brian shouted. "Mr. Andrews! We're friends," Brian said, his face heated up to a million degrees. He wasn't sure why he had shouted, but it got her attention.

"That so?" Ms. Trendy-turned-suspicious asked, then punched in a few digits before stating, "Mr. Andrews, I'm sorry to bother you. But you have a visitor. A Mr.?" She turned to stare at Brian, who answered, "Brian. Brian

Kelly!"

Suddenly, Ms. Trendy-turned-polite-once-more answered what must've been a question from Everett. "Yessir, all right, sir, I will tell him." She hung up the phone and pointed wordlessly at the hallway.

"So I'll go that way until I hit his door?"

"Mmmmhmmmm," Ms. Trendy-now-aloof replied before flopping back in her chair. She picked up noise-canceling headphones to let Brian know he was dismissed and swiveled to start pecking away at her keyboard.

Brian walked down the hallway and knocked on Everett's door, trying to hold back a grin as he imagined his old friend's reaction.

"Brian!" Everett's ruddy face broke into a broad grin when he appeared at the door. "How good to see you. What are you doing here?"

"It's so good to see you, too. Running the place now, are you?"

Everett laughed and gave a little shrug.

"Well, I won't keep you long," Brian said. "I'm kinda here for a weird reason. I'm not sure if you knew, but Alan and Claire Kendall—who works here—were engaged before his death."

The look on Everett's face told Brian he did not know any of what he had sprung on him.

"I'm so sorry," Everett said in a somber tone.

Brian smiled weakly. "When we lost Alan, Claire and I stayed connected, just chatting now and then. I wanted to surprise her and send her flowers—you know just to cheer her up—but I don't have her address." Brian hesitated, then said earnestly, "Actually, I was hoping to go see her. It's been a while."

"She's a lovely girl. I'm sure she'd welcome a visit! Speaking of, you should come around more often."

"I'm trying to resume somewhat of a normal life. It's been going better," Brian said in a halting manner. "I'd really appreciate her address. You have my honor. I'm not a stalker."

"Oh, shut up, Bub!" Everett boomed, using Brian's long-buried college nickname. That got Brian rolling, and Everett invited him into his office, where they small-talked a little more, promised to hang out again soon, and Everett pushed a business card with an address scrawled on the back at him. "Here you go. Give Claire my best, and tell her to hurry up and get back here!" Everett chuckled. "Honestly, we miss her. She sure does brighten up the place."

Brian nodded and tucked the card into his pocket. He thanked Everett and headed for the door, his stomach in his throat at the thought of seeing Claire again. All of a sudden, he felt so exposed and foolish. *Maybe Claire doesn't even feel the same way?*

༒

Claire inhaled deeply, sitting on one of the two wicker chairs Chloe had placed on her lovely front porch. The air was tranquil and scented with lilacs—a scent that transported Claire back to her childhood and playing in her grandmother's rambling backyard, Chloe right beside her. She remembered holding sticky orange popsicles in her hands and feeling the sun's rays on her hair. She laid her head on the back of the chair and closed her eyes.

That May morning was truly special. As Claire sipped her decaf coffee and took in the beautiful weather, she realized how truly fortunate she was to be there with Chloe and her family. She only had a few more months to go before the baby was born, and she her stomach had popped out even more that morning. Now she wore as many maternity dresses as she could. The baby was getting bigger every day it seemed, and her feet swelled now and then. She had read, in her many pregnancy books, about everything she might experience. Claire drowsed in and out of her thoughts about the past, present, and future. Her pulse picked up a little when she imagined being alone with just the baby and Chloe at home hundreds of miles away.

But she had to consider all that was ahead. When she returned home to her apartment in Chicago, could she keep living there with a baby and then a small child? Would she be expected to return to work each morning, or could she still work from home some of the time? If she had to, could she find a reputable nanny to care for her baby? Claire picked her head up off the back of the chair and took a sip of her coffee. *Don't lose your head and get too far down the path*, she directed herself. *You will figure it all out.* She set her coffee cup back down on the table. *You have no choice.*

Suddenly a car pulled up, and stopped directly in front of the house. A man got out and, then, as he moved closer to her on the front porch, Claire realized with her pulse throbbing in her throat, it was BRIAN! *Oh, my God.* Her arms made a protective cradle around her stomach. *What is he doing here?*

As Brian approached the porch steps, he smiled and said, "Surprise, Claire! How are you?"

Claire's heart raced as she pulled herself out of her reverie. "I—I'm fine," Claire stuttered. Her eyes went inadvertently to her belly. "What brings you here?"

"I talked to your boss, Everett Andrews, a former college pal, by the way, and he gave me your address. I hope that was okay. I have been thinking about you so much and wondering how you are doing. By the looks of things, am I going to be an uncle?"

Claire was horrified to feel tears prickle behind her eyes. Brian's smile disappeared, and a look of concern replaced it.

"No, no, Brian," Claire said red-faced and still stuttering, "I, uh, well, I am not having Alan's baby. The timing would be all wrong anyway."

"Oh!" The light in Brian's eyes dimmed. "I mean, of course I knew that. Just making terrible conversation." He sat down in the chair next to Claire. "I didn't know you were seeing anyone, but I never asked …"

"I'm not!"

"Well, yes, that's your business. I just feel a little silly."

"For visiting me?" Claire's heart hadn't slowed since the second she'd laid eyes on Brian. She felt suddenly breathless.

"Brian, it's a very long and terrible story. That's why I haven't told you. I should have, but I was so worried …" Claire hung her head and hid behind a silky drape of hair. "I only shared my news with two friends, hoping to keep it quiet. I hope you will forgive me and that I didn't hurt your feelings. Would you like a cup of coffee?"

"Thank you, no. I had a to-go cup of coffee on the drive down here, and I guess I'd better to-go back." Brian's lame joke fell flat as Claire tried to figure out how he was really feeling. Whatever warmth he had exuded before had extinguished, like a match blown out.

"Please sit down, Brian," Claire said, and took his hand. It was warm and strong in hers. She let out raggedly, "You deserve to hear the truth. As shocking as it is, I will tell the entire story to you now."

Brian's visage changed to concern as he stared her in the eyes. They were still holding hands, neither one making an effort to let go.

Claire sighed and told Brian the story all the way from the beginning. She didn't spare any of the awful details even when she started crying, and his grip on her hand tightened. The wrinkles in Brian's brow deepened as her storytelling went on.

When she finished, she leaned forward and dabbed her eyes with the hem of her long dress. Brian stood up and paced the porch.

"Claire, this is horrible, hideous, and totally despicable. What a lousy excuse for a man. I cannot tell you how sorry I am to learn all this, and my heart is breaking for the suffering you have endured. Please, please, what can I do to help you?" Brian asked, turning to her, his voice cracking with emotion. "I want to help you. Please let me help. I will do anything."

A small smile played on Claire's lips as she murmured, "Thank you, Brian. There is really nothing anyone can do. I appreciate the offer. I must admit, even though I have Chloe, her family, and my two closest friends, I feel very alone. I miss Alan more each day."

Tears trickled down Claire's cheek. "This is all so unfair, and while I can't wait to meet this little boy, there isn't a moment that is pure happiness." Brian nodded as he faced Claire on the other side of the porch. She had never seen his eyes exude such compassion. "Alan and I talked about having a family. He wanted a bunch of kids, and I was happy to see him so excited at the thought of it." Claire wiped her cheeks with the heels of her hands. "When do you think I will stop being so sad, Brian?"

"I ask myself that every day," Brian replied softly. "I've lived with him from the moment of conception. Learning to live without him has been like learning to survive without a vital organ."

"Of course!" Claire soothed and rushed to him. "I haven't been there for you as much as I should have. Oh, Brian, I am so sorry. I wish I could bring him back for you."

"I wish the same for you, Claire." Brian's voice was low as he swept her into his arms. They stayed that way for a while, just swaying on the porch.

Then Brian pulled back, and Claire was elated to see the twinkle in his eyes was back. "What are your plans for the rest of the day? Do you have any appointments, anything that you need to attend to? I will take you wherever you need to go."

"Nope, I don't have anything going on today. But would you like to take a drive around town? I could show you all the best points of interest," smiled Claire.

"Yes, I would like that. I also would like to take to you to dinner tonight. Just the two of us, if that is agreeable with you," Brian said with an anxious twist in his voice. "That would be nice, thank you," said Claire. *Why do I sound like a pioneer girl accepting a gentleman caller? Relax, girl!* Aloud she said, "Let me run in and grab my purse, and we can go. I would introduce you to the rest of the family, but no one's home right now. Later." She smiled at him and went inside.

When she came out, Brian was sitting in the chair again. Claire glanced at his ankles and giggled. "Violins! I love it!" *It's sure nice to know some things never change.* Brian stood up and offered his arm, and Claire took it as he went overboard, trying to help her down the steps. "I'm pregnant, not a Fabergé egg, goofy!" she teased him as his cheeks heated up.

"Oh, yes, I know. It's just you're precious cargo."

"Aw, Brian," was all she could get out. The rest of the words stuck in a blissful ball in her throat.

The short drive around town was uneventful and filled with Claire asking questions about Brian's life.

"Are you busy at work?" "Have you been feeling well?" "Have you been out socially?" "Any new friends?" Brian answered each question as Claire fired them off, and he couldn't help but grin and laugh in between sharing what was going on in his life.

When the tour was over, Claire announced, "Brian, I had better get home. I am still working each day for your friend, Everett, ah, Mr. Andrews. I can't have him disappointed in me and fire me. God knows I need this job."

"Everett adores you, silly," Brian said.

He walked Claire to the front door with the promise he would be back to pick her up for their dinner date promptly at five o'clock.

Claire blushed as she told him, "I'm looking forward to our date, Brian, and I'll be ready."

Brian plucked up her hand from her side, planted a soft kiss on the top of it, and walked down the steps whistling.

Chapter 15

The first thing Brian did when he was back in his car was find the nicest restaurant nearby. He decided on Epiphany Farms on Front Street in Bloomington, hoping for a memorable evening with Claire.

When they were seated at the best table in the restaurant (Brian's request to the host, accompanied by a nice tip), Claire looked around and with an approving smile, said, "This is so lovely, Brian. I have never been here before." They ordered drinks—a decaf cola for Claire, a red wine for Brian. When Brian asked Claire if she would mind if he ordered dinner for both of them, Claire's mind immediately went back to her romantic evenings with Alan. *I have to stop that*, thought Claire. *It isn't fair to Brian or me.* "I'd love that, please," she replied, ordering her nostalgic feelings to take a hike.

The dinner and the evening went well. Brian's company was effortless; a special energy accompanied their time together. How much they had admired and liked each other before was ignited into emotions neither could push away. When Brian brought Claire back to Chloe's, he thanked her for spending time with him and asked if it would be okay if he came down for another visit before the baby was born.

Claire held her hand on her heart, moonlight in her hair and stars in her eyes. "I would love that so much," she whispered. Brian leaned over and kissed her on the cheek.

The corners of Claire's mouth went up just a little, and she realized *there is still so much to be grateful for, even during the uncertain times*. Instead of living in the past and lamenting who wasn't here anymore, she would focus on who was and who would soon be. Now she was feeling hope, blooming and breaking open like all the spring flowers surrounding her. As Brian climbed into his car and drove away, Claire waved until he disappeared over the horizon. Her heart ached at seeing him go. That's when she knew she was in trouble.

❧

The early summer months slipped by with Claire working and still feeling good—although she grew increasingly uncomfortable as her tummy bulged and the baby lodged under her ribs. Nowadays, she waddled more than walked. Of course, there were all the usual miseries of pregnancy: insomnia, night sweats, hemorrhoids, and sore joints, just to name a few. But the closer she got to holding her baby, the further from her mind the rape seemed. Her baby was feeling more and more like an immaculate conception. And on the heels of that, she couldn't help thinking, *thank God, Bryce is dead.* It was a horrifying thought, but Claire let herself feel what she needed to. The truth was, if Bryce had survived, she had to wonder how safe she and her baby would be. Karma had a way of sorting out the worst problems. And now, she would do whatever she could to ensure her baby never found out the truth. *All you will ever know, my sweet prince, is that you are so very adored and wanted.*

Chloe and her family still loved and catered to Claire even though so many months had passed that it would have been natural for the bloom to fall off that rose. Mr. Andrews wanted her back at work, but he understood when Claire told him that Chloe had suffered some complications, making her recovery lag a little. "It's a good thing you're on top of your work," Mr. Andrews exclaimed in his usual booming voice. "Please give your sister my best."

"Thank God for Chloe and all the love and care she has showered on me," Claire said aloud, "and thank God for Mr. Andrews!" Then she scolded herself for straying from the tasks at hand and got back to work.

❧

Scotty's doctors were at a loss to figure out why his convulsions and erratic behavior were still so prevalent. The medication they administered should have relieved more of his symptoms, but it didn't.

Scotty would rant and yell at the top of his lungs, usually in the middle of the night. He seemed a little more passive during the day, but sometimes he would become irritated, and his unholy hollering would begin. It was apparent that Scotty was becoming increasingly ill, and the doctors didn't know how to help him.

One day, he was moved to a more secure part of the hospital where he could scare the other patients with his outbursts.

☙

As soon as Brian got home, he called Claire. Then he started phoning once or twice a week, and before long, the calls increased to three to four times a week, not to mention all the texting in between. He was planning another trip to visit her, and when he told Claire about it, she was delighted at how happy that made her feel.

When Brian did drive down, they went on long walks and settled into equally long talks. The more and more time they spent together, the more comfortable they got with each other. August was nearing, and with that, a new baby would arrive.

On one walk, hand in hand, Brian stopped in the middle of a path, turned to Claire, and took her other hand. As they faced each other, he smiled down at her and said, "Claire, please let me be there for the delivery. I would love that more than anything, to be in the room as that little one takes their first breath."

Claire grinned back up at him and chuckled, "It's not like I can control it!"

Brian laughed, too, and Claire assured him she would do her best to make sure he was there. Then she gave him a big squeeze and a kiss on his scruffy cheek.

"I know you can't be so exact," Brian said when she pulled away, "but please keep me in the loop every day, and let me know any news about how you are feeling and if you think the baby is coming. I can always stay at a hotel in Normal for a week or two."

But there was no time for that. As Claire had stated, babies and deliveries are unpredictable. Dr. Blakely told Claire at her next appointment that the baby's blood pressure had plummeted. "We need to take your baby via C-section right now," she told a worried Claire, whose heart was racing overtime.

Now Claire was thrust into fresh new fears. *Will my baby be all right?*

Things moved quickly. After a brief call to Chloe and Brian, Claire was taken to the delivery room. Nurses helped Claire into a hospital gown and back onto the gurney. She was whisked off to the operating room, where Dr. Blakely gave her an epidural. Claire would be awake for the delivery but would not feel any pain. It wasn't pain that she cared about. After everything she and her baby had gone through, she couldn't imagine leaving the hospital without him or her in her arms. On the table, a degree away from hysteria, she clamped down on her feelings and focused on breathing deeply.

Tears rolled down Claire's face as Dr. Blakely worked to get the baby out. She wondered *where is Chloe? Where is Brian?* She repeatedly prayed for someone to be there to hold her hand as she remembered their words. Chloe had reassured her, "Deliveries are scary. Everything will be okay!" Brian had said, "I'm walking to the car and headed straight to you. I'll be right there. You aren't doing this alone."

By some miracle, Chloe made it before Claire's baby was out. She was even allowed to be in the room and witness the birth, as long as she could control herself and handle being in the OR, the surgical team said with serious expressions. Chloe assured them she was a birthing veteran.

Claire's mind spun with what could have gone wrong for the baby's blood pressure to drop. She trembled as she tried to figure out, *what brought all of this on? Are both of us going to be all right?* With those fears circling Claire's mind, suddenly, she heard the baby's cry. "Oh my God, is the baby okay?" Claire asked. She was so afraid that she almost didn't recognize her own voice.

"Claire, *he* is perfect!" Chloe said. Dr. Blakely agreed. "Right as rain and a beautiful son you have here!"

As soon as Dr. Blakely cut the cord and the nurses cleaned him up, a nurse plopped Claire's perfect pink baby on her chest. Claire ran her eyes all over his body and face, taking in everything. His head full of dark hair and his wrinkled red face. He *was* perfect, with the right number of fingers and toes. Despite their little health scare, he appeared to be a very healthy newborn. Dr. Blakely informed Claire that she would stay in the hospital for two or three days because of the cesarean section. His heart rate had dropped due to cord compression. "He'll have no lasting issues," Dr. Blakely said, squeezing Claire's shoulder.

Claire didn't mind the extra time to rest; she had so much to sort out. *First of all, what about a name for this little guy?* On the heels of her euphoria was the dimmer thought, *poor little baby, it's not his fault his father was such a creep. Will I ever be able to just love him and forget his horrible conception? I certainly will try*, Claire thought as her nameless baby boy was taken away while she was stitched up.

In the meantime, Brian had arrived and was impatiently waiting in the lobby. When he was finally allowed to see Claire, he stared down at her in the bed, his eyes glossy with tears. "You did it, yay," he said in a hush. He leaned over very gently to hug Claire and whispered in her ear, "I am so proud of you." Then he brushed a kiss on her cheek as Claire positively beamed and flushed in joy.

Brian straightened up. "Now, let me see that little man!" He made his way over to the bassinet and stood gazing at the baby. "You make beautiful babies, Claire," he said over his shoulder. "May I hold him?" Claire nodded with a sleepy smile. She couldn't keep her eyes open any longer. "Brian, if you've got the baby, I might just take a little catnap?"

"Of course," Brian cooed. He carefully picked up the baby and settled into a rocking chair in the corner of the room. When he peeked at Claire, she was already asleep.

After a few days in the hospital and clear check-ups for both mother and baby, it was time to return to Chloe's and heal up before Claire, and the baby, returned home. Lou decided to postpone his business trip to see if he could be of any help in bringing Claire and the baby home. He was rather anxious to meet the newest member of the family, too, as were Michael and Melissa—who waited as patiently as they could with the nanny.

Claire was tired, but so happy with all the shouts of approval. Stifling back laughter, she told her niece and nephew to "Use our inside voices, please. He's very sleepy right now." Then she winked to let them know she understood their excitement. They snapped their mouths shut as they stood there with bright eyes at their brand-new cousin. She had to admit, their raves of "Oh, he is adorable," and "THE cutest baby EVER!" made her so proud.

After talking it over with Chloe and the family, her baby had a name. Daniel Alan Kendall.

Claire figured probably she and everyone else would end up calling him Danny. She hoped that Alan would feel honored at having a sort-of namesake, and maybe he was even smiling down at her. The edges of Brian's grin nearly reached his ears when he heard Danny's middle name. He also admitted that "Daniel is a strong Irish name. Very fitting." And then, as had happened through that whole year as they both tried to get used to life without Alan, Brian's voice caught with tears. Claire's heart went out to him. She knew exactly how he felt. It was such an odd feeling to love someone so deeply while also falling in love with another. But that's exactly where she was in her life.

Brian visited every day from the nearby hotel where he stayed. He had rescheduled his patients' appointments as he didn't want to miss a moment of this joyous time with Claire and her family. Also, he definitely agreed with Melissa and Michael that "Danny is the cutest baby, EVER!" That exclamation sent the kids into peals of laughter as they scampered off into the house.

After about a week, with Claire feeling stronger every day, she announced she was ready to go home. It was time, and as much as she hated leaving Chloe and her family, she had to face the uncertainty ahead.

To ease the transition into new mommyhood, she had hired a nanny to help with Danny while she worked from home. But in the back of her mind, a thought nagged: *What if Mr. Andrews insists I return to work in the office?* She tried her best to take this new situation one step at a time. *I'll just deal with it if that is his decision, but I don't know anything or what he's thinking … and I'm not even home yet. I've gotta calm down!*

Besides getting into a new groove and seeing Brian as much as she could, she was so anxious to see Ellie and Vida. She packed and cooed at Danny as he lay there in his bassinet.

Vida and Ellie couldn't wait to be reunited with Claire, and meet young Danny, too. In between squeals on the phone, they insisted they were both available to babysit anytime she needed.

Claire couldn't imagine leaving her brand-new baby for even a minute, but she filed away the thought in the back of her mind.

Chapter 16

The August day that Claire and Danny would return home was extremely hot. Claire donned one of her short-sleeve shifts she'd worn in her early pregnancy. She had wanted to put on something not labeled "maternity wear," but she told herself she was being silly. *So what if it's a maternity dress? Anything to feel comfortable.* With her incision still healing, she couldn't wear tight clothes anyway.

Brian placed Danny in the car seat since Claire was on a lifting restriction for another few weeks. She leaned over Danny and tucked in the navy plaid blanket Chloe had bought for him. The significance of her older sister buying her baby his first blanket was not lost on Claire. Danny represented a huge milestone in her life—and she supposed Brian did, too. Traveling back to Chicago with him and the baby in the back felt completely natural. If she considered it long enough, she could almost convince herself he was the father. *Whoa, tiger,* she ordered herself, smiling slightly.

"Are you going to share the joke with me?" Brian asked, a smile on his face too.

"Oh!" Claire jumped in her seat. She really had been lost in a world of her own making.

Brian laid his hand on hers. "Just so you know what's going on in my head, I'm just happy to be taking my two favorite people home."

At that, Claire positively melted, and her heart beat so loud, she was surprised it didn't explode out of her ears.

Brian led the way in the small caravan of cars accompanying Danny and Claire back to Chicago. Lou followed Brian in Claire's car, and Chloe followed close behind in her car. The kids were with a sitter, despite their loud protests.

Danny had no idea of the excitement surrounding him. Like a trooper, he slept all the way home.

When Brian put the key in the door of Claire's apartment, Danny in his car seat firmly in the grip of his hand, Claire walked into the home she hadn't returned to in months. Her eyes swept the room. "What is all this?" She gestured to the dozens of roses bursting in bloom everywhere she looked.

Brian shrugged, his cheeks flushing. "Well, it's a pretty momentous occasion. You and Danny deserve the best homecoming."

Ellie had even slipped over earlier and turned on the air conditioning full blast. Claire wasn't sure what she was happier about, the adoration Brian poured onto her and Danny, or that she wasn't sweating out of her dress.

Claire drifted around the living room, running her fingers over her couch, tables, and chairs. "Ahhhh, my home. I really did miss it!"

Brian responded with a chuckle and a gleam in his eye. Chloe just smiled as Lou brought in more bags.

After a solid feeding and unpacking Danny's things, Brian ordered dinner for four. Within the hour, they were dining on chicken parmesan, salads, and even cannoli. Everyone was hungrier than they realized. Brian had done so much for Claire since all this had happened, so very much. She couldn't help stealing glances at him throughout dinner. Every time they caught each other's eyes, they giggled until Chloe joked, "You two sure have a case of puppy love!" Then seeming to realize what she'd said, she quickly gulped her wine before adding, "I'm sorry, but it had to be said."

"It did," Brian said in his warm, deep voice that made Claire's belly do flips.

"Here, let me hold him," Chloe said to Claire, her arms extended to receive the baby from Claire, who had been juggling eating and holding him. "I'm already missing him!"

Claire put Danny in Chloe's arms. "Don't get any ideas," Lou said around a mouthful of pasta. "We're all full up at the inn!"

"I know," Chloe said softly. "Babies are certainly intoxicating!"

After dinner, Chloe and Lou left for home. Claire hated to say goodbye. She blinked back tears as she shut the door behind them. Brian stood behind her, Danny sound asleep in his arms. "Let me put this little guy down for his nap," Claire cooed at Brian and Danny both. Brian smiled and handed the baby over. "I could get used to this."

She winked at Brian and turned down the hallway to put Danny in his crib. "This is your home now, little one," murmured Claire as she laid him down. "I hope you like it."

When Claire emerged from the bedroom, Brian opened his arms for a hug and a heavenly soft kiss on the lips. Claire did not hold back this time. She loved having him there in her life and, as weird as it sounded, she felt that Alan would want this for the two of them.

"Beautiful lady," Brian tipped her chin up, so she was staring into his blazing baby blues. "I know you have got to be so tired, so I am going to take off for tonight. I insist you go sit on the couch while I clean all this up, but I will call you tomorrow if that's okay?"

Claire's mouth fell open. "I can't let you clean all this up!" But Brian shushed her and led her to the couch. "Get comfy," he insisted as he tucked a throw blanket around her. "It's important for you to rest not only for Danny, but you're still healing. Please humor me?"

Claire reluctantly agreed, and Brian walked off whistling to do the dishes and wipe down the table and counters. Then he said his goodbyes with another longer kiss that stole Claire's breath. When they broke apart, Brian smiled down at her and shook his head. "Wow," he whispered as he made his way to the door.

Her head still spinning, Claire called Ellie to tell her she was home and ask if there was any news about the office.

"I am so happy you're home! How's the baby doing?" Ellie replied, ignoring Claire's question. Claire chuckled silently to herself. Ellie was a sucker for babies, and she would be an even bigger sucker for Danny—she knew it already.

"He's being an angel so far. I just put him down, and he's sleeping like he's lived in the nursery all his life. Let's hope that continues."

After a few more words, Claire yawned in the middle of a sentence. "I knew it!" Ellie said. "I'll let you go, and don't worry. I'll call Vida and tell her you're home. Maybe we can figure out the best time for us to come over? We are so anxious to see you and meet our new precious love. And about the office, nothing really new. Nothing like what you have going on." They hung up, the smile in Ellie's voice still echoing in Claire's ears. *Little Danny, you are the luckiest baby to have such loving aunts!*

The next day, Ellie and Vida arrived and took turns holding and feeding Danny. They both agreed that he was an exceptionally adorable boy.

Vida, who Claire had thought wasn't as much of a homebody as Ellie, was clearly in love.

"Vida, didn't you hear my question? I asked if everything at the office is going along as before."

"Office, smoffice," Vida said, not breaking eye contact with Danny.

"Vida!" Claire protested, but it was in good fun. She was delighted that Vida appeared to be in love.

"Fine," Vida swiveled her head to answer Claire. She pulled Danny in closer to her and popped his pacifier in his mouth.

"Nothing too newsy, thank goodness," Vida elaborated, "except we heard that Scotty was confined to a special hospital. Not sure how long he will be there or if he can ever leave again. Hopefully, he's permanently indisposed." She said the last part in baby talk.

Claire felt her eyebrows shoot up almost to the middle of her forehead. "Scotty will always be a threat hanging over my head. After all this time, I wish I could stop worrying that he'll figure out what happened and blab it all over the place." She got up from her dining room table, where the three of them nursed drinks.

"What would happen if the truth of Bryce's death became public knowledge? Would I be prosecuted? Would I lose all respect with my friends and coworkers?" Anguish stole over Claire's face. Ellie jumped up from her chair and put an arm around Claire's shoulders. "It is always in the back of my mind," Claire said, shaking her head. "I am never free of feeling so anxious."

"Try not to think about Scotty right now, Claire, or ever," Ellie said, understanding in her voice. "If his mind is so cloudy and mixed up, no matter what he might have to say, would people believe him?"

"I agree," Vida chimed in softly, looking up from tending Danny. "He was so off the wall; I doubt anyone would believe his wild and crazy stories."

"I hope you're both right," Claire sighed.

"Come sit back down, and let's finish our visit without letting memories of Scotty ruin it," Ellie said soothingly. She led Claire back to her chair at the table, and the conversation took a better turn. The star of the show was Danny, and the ladies adjusted their focus to him and how adorable and perfect he was.

Before they all knew it, three hours had passed, and Vida gasped when she looked at her phone. "Girlfriend," Vida directed at Claire, "you need your rest. Come on, El, it's time to call it a day."

Ellie rose from her chair and walked over to hug Claire. "She's right. Please, both of you, take a nap."

"That's the plan," Claire said. She was glad Vida had noticed the time because suddenly, she could hardly keep her eyes open.

"Danny is so adorable, Claire," Ellie said and kissed Claire's cheek. "I hope he brings years of joy to you. God knows you deserve it."

"You better look out," grinned Vita. "I may just try and steal him from you. I'm smitten already."

The next morning Claire fed, changed, and placed Danny in his crib. She waited until she was sure he was asleep, then crept out to the couch and called Mr. Andrews.

After exchanging the usual pleasantries, Claire explained that she was back home, along with an apology for being away so long.

"Well, Claire, I am happy to hear that. We certainly missed you, though I must say that you did one heck of a great job while at your sister's. By the way, how is she doing now?"

"Thank you for asking. Chloe is much better, and her husband is going to cut back on his business travel. So all's well. I do have something to ask you, if I may?"

"Of course." Mr. Andrews said.

"Well, I am wondering what your thoughts are as far as my working from home or coming back to work in the office?" Claire inquired.

"It's funny you should ask that, Claire. Your flex schedule and your productivity have helped us launch a new initiative at the office. We are trying out a part-time remote arrangement with several other people and will be glad to extend this to you. Of course, I don't mean that you aren't in the office a couple of days a week, but maybe you could work three days from home—whatever days would suit the work best. Thanks for being that inspiration for this project. I am starting to be of the mind that in some cases, people seem to do a better job when they have fewer distractions."

"This sounds wonderful," Claire said, trying not to sound relieved. "It's absolutely perfect. Thank you, Mr. Andrews! I will give you my best and hope I will make you happy with your decision."

"It's settled then," Mr. Andrews said. "Figure out which days you will work in the office and which days are best for you to work at home, and let's talk tomorrow. Just give me a call when you've made your decision."

Claire could not believe her good fortune. Her anxiety about handling work with a new baby was slowly dissipating.

But just as soon as one worry wrapped up, she was off to another. *When should I start looking for a house with a yard for Danny? When should I buy a high chair?* A million questions plagued her when it came to raising him right. *Welcome to motherhood,* she thought with an exasperated smile.

Claire chose the office days as Monday and Friday. With the three days in the middle of the week at home, she could really knuckle down and compound her energy.

Next, she set about to find a nanny. After interviewing a few duds, Claire found Margie. She was a lovely, caring girl with a background in nursing, which delighted Claire.

Margie hit it off with Danny immediately. And for the second time that week, Claire was relieved.

In the meantime, her burgeoning feelings for Brian and his two kisses wouldn't leave her mind. *Especially that last one!*

Brian called every day, wanting to know how she and Danny were getting along, if they needed anything, and what the new work arrangement would be. "I hope you have good news for me!" Brian said, and Claire's stomach turned acrobatics.

"Things are working out beautifully! Better than I imagined. But one thing needs a little work."

"What's that?" Brian asked, all eager beaver.

"Danny and I miss you and would love to have a visit."

"Does he? Well, we can't have that. I miss you both so much. How about this Saturday? Shall I bring dinner?"

"Please don't go to any trouble. We can order something, since I am not quite up to cooking just yet. Does that sound okay?"

"Anything sounds more than okay!" grinned Brian through the other end of the phone.

The evening went well. All three participants were happy and peaceful. Danny was a good baby and proved it without a lot of fussing or crying, Claire and Brian enjoyed their time together, and when they weren't passing Danny back and forth, they mostly spent the night mooning over each other, teasing, flirting, and making excuses to touch each other. A few lingering fingers on an arm here, a tucking away of hair behind Claire's ear there. Every time she felt Brian's touch, her infatuation with him grew. *Because it's not love, right?*

The night ended too soon with Danny put to bed and Claire and Brian lingering by the door with another kiss that shot off fireworks.

"That never gets old," Brian said as he inched closer to the door, Claire on his arm. "I can't wait to see you again."

"Me neither," Claire whispered, standing on her tippy-toes to peck him on the lips once more. "One for the road." Claire shrugged as Brian scooped her into his arms again and laid another kiss on her. Eventually, they parted, clothes a little askew, silly grins on their faces. "Goodnight, angel," Brian said, and shut the door behind him.

Chapter 17

Claire found she liked the idea of being in the office a couple of days a week. She'd always enjoyed spending time with her best friends, and it felt good to be out among other employees. Not that she wasn't completely in love with Danny—because she was.

Life had hit a new groove, and Claire had all the hope in the world that the worst was behind her. With Danny, she knew the best was in front of her.

One day a young man appeared at the office, claiming he was a good friend of Scotty's. He had black, slicked-back hair, a long pointy nose, and a thin mustache. Vida thought he resembled a villain. Claire wasn't at work when Scotty's friend came in, but she sure heard about it later.

"Scotty and I go way back. We have stayed friends for all these years. My mother used to say, 'Jonathan, I swear you and Scotty are joined at the hip.'" Vida hoped Jonathan would get to the point. Any mention of Scotty made her lose her appetite.

"I still keep in touch with Scotty," Jonathan drawled on, having no idea how badly Vida wanted to escape. *I'd even head back to that department meeting*, she thought.

Jonathan was clueless as he prattled on, "Poor guy dealing with this illness. I know he will get better, and someday we will be able to go out and grab some beers, maybe even take in a Cub's game."

"Why are you here?" Vida barged into the conversation, suspecting this dimwit would never leave if she didn't.

Jonathan drilled hard, cold eyes into Vida's startled ones. He spoke slowly with annoyance. "Scotty said he had a notebook of some kind that should still be in his locker. He asked if I would pick it up for him and bring it to the hospital. Do you have any idea where I might find that?"

"I can see if his locker is unlocked. If not, Mr. Andrews has a key." She felt a chill creep down her spine. *What the hell had Scotty written in a journal? And why keep it at work? Don't get all paranoid,* she chided herself, *it's probably just a bunch of gibberish.*

Scotty's locker was indeed locked, so Vida had to enlist Mr. Andrews's help. The three of them went to the locker, which meant there was no chance of Vita sneaking a peek at whatever Scotty's deranged mind had conjured up.

The journal in hand, Jonathan thanked them both and flashed a sickening grin.

"Scotty is going to be very happy." Jonathan rocked back on his heels. "He made it sound like there was some heavy info in this journal. I'll see he gets it right away."

Vida hated the thought of telling Claire what had just happened, but she knew she had to call her just the same.

Once Jonathan had left, Vida returned to her desk and dialed Claire's number on her cell phone.

Claire listened carefully as Vida explained the story. When Vida stopped talking, she said, "Wow, this could be really bad news or nothing to worry about. We just don't know how lucid Scotty is. He might have written everything down when he was more cognizant. God, will this nightmare ever end?"

Vida did her best to reassure her, but she didn't know if it would ever end either. Just when life had gotten back on track, Scotty had to pop up. It angered her more than anything.

☙

Jonathan couldn't wait to read what was so damned important in the journal. He went through it, keeping his opinions to himself, knowing Scotty would kill him if he knew. And also knowing, after what he read, that Scotty was more than capable of doing it.

That week, Jonathan showed up at the hospital to visit Scotty.

"Bro, what the hell took you so long?" Scotty asked from his hospital bed. Jonathan tried to ignore the restraints that shackled Scotty down and the big dude standing outside the door who looked like he would kick both their asses. Scotty twitched and asked, a weird intensity in his eyes, "Did you get my journal?"

"I got it from your locker, but this stupid hospital wouldn't let me bring it in. No journal, no diaries, etc. Sorry, dude."

"What the shit does that mean?" yelled Scotty. "You didn't read it, did you?"

"No, of course not. You told me not to."

"I can't believe these idiotic rules!" Scotty hollered, and the mountain of the man outside the door poked his head inside the room. "Watch the volume," he growled. Silence ensued, and Jonathan had no idea what to say. All he knew was that Scotty's room felt ice cold.

"Are you thinking of blackmailing this Claire gal?" asked Jonathan. As soon as the words were out of his mouth, he realized his mistake.

"You worm. You lowlife. I thought you said you didn't read it! I knew you did." Scotty hissed. He snapped his head toward the door looking for the mountain man, Jonathan suspected. He was very thankful for the large man's presence and the restraints that were doing their job as Scotty attempted to charge at him.

"Don't get your skivvies in a knot. I won't tell anybody what you're planning to do," grinned Jonathan. "You're one sick puppy, though."

Scotty's mind went into overdrive. "Why don't you go back to your rat's nest of a house and get out of here?"

Jonathan smirked. "You sure got steamed over a few pages. I can't figure out why, or maybe I can ..."

"Get out!" Scotty screamed. This time, the security guard did come barreling into the room. "I told you," he warned as he headed toward Scotty's bed. Jonathan scampered out of there as fast as he could. Scotty's cries of "Nooooo!" and "I'm sorry! I'll behave!" echoed down the hallway. He turned back to glance at Scotty's door and saw other staff racing toward his room. Jonathan shook his head and pledged never to return. *Childhood friendship or not, Scotty's lost it!*

☙

The brief mention of Scotty appeared to be a fluke. Months passed with Claire marveling at how well her life was working out and the feelings of contentment she was experiencing. Danny was thriving and healthy and happy. She thanked God every day for that.

She and Brian were falling in love. He made her so happy the way he always tried to take care of her and Danny, bouncing him around as he called him "my little man." And Claire let him, even though they weren't a family yet. In the back of her mind, she hoped for it, while wondering if she wanted it so much because she wanted a father for Danny more than she loved Brian. Then she chased that thought away. It was ridiculous. No matter how Brian had come into their lives, he was meant to be—with her and with Danny.

Even her work was humming right along. She'd taken the lead on several marketing projects, and her performance review was excellent. For the first time in a long time, she relaxed into her life instead of preparing to go to battle.

It was Mother's Day, and as silly as it sounded, Claire wanted to look nice for Danny. *He needs to see his mommy looking good.* As Claire looked in the mirror to apply her favorite lipstick, Mauve Gloss, her image appeared cloudy. She pulled her sleeve over her hand and wiped the mirror, but nothing was on it. She didn't think too much of it and returned to putting on her lipstick. *It'll work its way out—whatever it is.*

☙

Jonathan was finishing his dinner when he heard a knock at his front door. When he looked through the peephole, he couldn't believe his eyes! "Scotty, what are you doing here?" Jonathan asked as he opened the door a crack, his head fuzzy with fear.

Scotty leaned into the door so it burst open. He caught himself before he fell onto the floor. "I came for my journal. Get it for me NOW!"

"You don't have to raise your voice and use that attitude with me," Jonathan said, then, meekly, "I'll get your damned journal."

He turned down the hallway, Scotty's footsteps thumping along behind him.

"How did you escape?"

"For Christ's sake, don't get so melodramatic with your stupid questions," Scotty snapped. "I didn't escape. I just walked out the door."

Jonathan found that dubious. He'd witnessed the level of security on the floor, but he didn't say anything. At his bedroom door, he stepped inside, and Scotty followed. Jonathan dug the journal out of his underwear drawer and handed it to Scotty.

"Ew, you're a freak. My journal touched your underwear. I should beat your ass for that."

Jonathan just shrugged, and Scotty took that as his cue to leave. With the journal under his arm, he hurried toward the front door. Then he turned and looked back at Jonathan. "Good thing you didn't put up a fuss. I brought a weapon in case you decided to get cute."

Jonathan's mouth gaped open. Understanding dawned in his eyes. "What the hell is the matter with you? What kind of weapon?"

"Well, nosey, I 'borrowed' a butcher knife from the hospital kitchen. Lucky for you, I didn't need to use it. Toodles." Scotty wiggled his fingers at him, then walked out the front door.

Jonathan watched him go, then scurried to the door and threw all the locks. He hoped that would be the last he would ever see of Scotty. Each time they'd gotten together, he'd been afraid there'd be one man left standing, and it wouldn't be him.

☙

Still wondering about her bleary eye, Claire did her best to carry on, telling herself she would get to the doctor when she could take the time. They'd just signed two new clients, and with all the consideration Mr. Andrews had extended her, she didn't feel like she could ask him to take the time off.

Claire finished feeding Danny, put him in his canvas sling chair, and made herself a cup of tea.

It was hard to concentrate on happy thoughts when she was worried about her vision—even if she wouldn't admit that to herself.

"No, not today. I am only going to be positive."

There was a lot to be positive about. Claire smiled, thinking back to the first time Brian had made love to her. She would never forget it or how fabulous it was.

Brian made me feel like I was the most beautiful woman in the world. The way his eyes surveyed my naked body said it all. He has to be the most caring, loving man in the world. It had only been a couple of weeks since they'd given in to their overwhelming passion. Claire had refused to compare him to Alan, but she'd worried that would be the case when the moment finally happened. But Brian was a separate person. She had to regard him that way. When the time finally came, none of those thoughts occurred. They were too intoxicated with each other to think of anything else.

Brian's kisses were sometimes tender and sometimes fierce! They had covered her face, neck, and her whole body. He took her to places higher than she had ever been—soaring to the heavens. Brian's arms held her as she floated back down to Earth.

The nap they'd shared afterwards had been about as great as the sex. Now Claire giggled, and Danny looked at her quizzically. He could see longer distances now, so she knew he could focus on her. "Hello, little nugget," she cooed. "Mommy loves you."

☙

Vida was standing at Ellie's desk engaging in a little water cooler talk when she suddenly looked up and said, "Uh-oh."

"What's the matter?" asked Ellie.

"Over there by the front door? It's that friend of Scotty's. He was here the other day and picked up Scotty's journal from his locker. I didn't think—well, I hoped—we would ever see him again."

Jonathan spotted Vida then and strolled over with his odd little walk.

"Hi gals! How's it going? Jonathan smiled like a robot, his eyes flat.

"I just thought you might be interested in a little excitement I had at my house last night."

"Why, what happened? I'm Ellie, by the way."

"Don't tell him your name," Vida hissed, then was immediately contrite. "I'm sorry, hun," she soothed at Ellie. "Why do we need to know this?" Vida demanded.

"I'll tell you what happened, and as unbelievable as it is, it's true. Scotty appeared at my front door in a very hostile mood. He said he came for his journal and had a knife with him in case there was trouble. I don't know if he went back to the hospital or where he might have gone. Just thought you would want to know."

"Do you think he went back to the hospital?" Vida asked anxiously.

"Did you happen to read the journal?" Ellie asked, alarm and curiosity in her eyes.

"It was mainly about a gal named Claire and a lady's compact Scotty had found. Didn't make much sense to me. But of course, Scotty isn't making much sense these days." Jonathan turned on his heel and flung "Well, bye," over his shoulder.

"That is one bizarre guy," Ellie said. Her eyes were huge as she was processing what it meant that Scotty was loose.

Vida chewed the inside of her cheek; then she spoke very slowly, "Do you think he is going to blackmail Claire, or worse?

"I don't think we can even imagine," Ellie sighed.

༄

Tucked away safe at home in her apartment, Claire had no idea that Scotty was loose. She hadn't seen Brian in a couple of days, and Danny was just getting over a cold. She was tired of being cooped up by herself. And then there was the issue with her eye. *Such a silly thing.* With no other symptoms, Claire convinced herself that she had scratched her cornea. *That must be it!* she thought brightly, and the thought lifted a weight that she hadn't realized had affected her so much.

Maybe it's time to get my act together and do a little entertaining. A small dinner party, with just my fave people, Claire thought. The prospect made her heart light. She couldn't wait to have everyone she loved most in the world under one roof again.

I'll call Brian, Ellie, and Vida. No one else. With my small dining area, that is about all I could fit anyway. She wished she could invite Chloe and her family, too, but school was in full swing, and Chloe was on her own with Lou traveling. But she knew Chloe would always be there. She was her best friend, and even when distance separated them, it was never in their hearts.

After inviting everyone, the date was set for the following Saturday evening.

On Saturday afternoon, Claire was busy setting the table. She had a fresh flower centerpiece and candles. She had even put Danny into a romper that looked like a suit. He was cuter than usual. *As if that's possible.* Claire smiled at him, and he smiled back, making her melt all the more.

Claire pulled on a new dress she had ordered online. It was a lovely pale blue with a V-neck, not too plunging, but just enough to make her look beautiful and sexy. She wanted Brian's eyes to fall out of his head.

Everyone was enjoying the evening, conversation, and wine. Brian got along so well with Ellie and Vida, which was important to Claire. She checked it off her list. *I guess he's perfect,* she thought with a secret smile.

Ellie broke into Claire's daydreaming. "It's so great of you to have all of us for dinner."

Claire waved her hand as if to excuse the comment. She clapped and said, "Okay, everyone, get to the table. I'm about to bring in the main event!" Then she disappeared into the kitchen amid murmurings of "I wonder what she made?" "I bet she's got some fancy steaks in there." "Maybe she made a soup?" That last remark had everyone laughing. "Soup?" Brian's voice rose out of the laughter, making Claire smile in the kitchen. She grinned through the smattering of conversation.

Claire picked up the pot roast swimming in carrots and potatoes on a silver platter and made her way to the kitchen door. As she stepped through to the dining room, she announced, "Get ready. I hope it's as good as it looks!"

She smiled at her friends and the loves of her life seated around the table, and everyone smiled back. As Claire carried the big platter to the table, a numbness suddenly gripped her arms, and she dropped the platter. Everyone was horrified. Claire sank to her knees on the white rug and started to cry. Brian jumped up and rushed to her. "Sweetheart, are you okay?"

The loud clatter woke Danny, and he started to cry. Ellie left the table to get him.

Claire was still inconsolable. Brian wiped her tears away and kissed her cheek. "Please don't be so upset. It's going to be okay."

"Something's wrong with me, Brian. I can feel it." Claire collapsed into his arms, crying harder as he tried to hug her pain away.

Chapter 18

Claire was not easily pacified about dropping the roast. She knew it wasn't her fault, and she'd gotten over being embarrassed as she sat there on the rug. Now her mind reeled to *why did it happen? What is going on?* Vida rushed over from her chair and sat beside Claire on the carpet. With Vida on one side and Brian on the other, they helped Claire to the couch. Her arms felt like dead weight, as if they'd disconnected from her body. Once she was settled on the couch, Vida reassuringly beside her, Brian set to work cleaning up the mess. Ellie bounced Danny and fed him when he got fussy.

A pall fell over the rest of the evening, as much as everyone tried to act as if nothing had happened. Everyone wanted to know if she needed to go to the emergency room. Claire dismissed that idea. "I'm fine. Whatever's going on can wait until the morning." Brian stayed near, concern masking his rugged face. The party departed earlier than usual at Brian's insistence that Claire needed her rest. Claire was so grateful for his authoritative presence. She was so tired that she could hardly sit up.

After Ellie and Vida left, Brian tried to console Claire. "Please sweetheart, don't keep thinking about the incident. Accidents happen, right? I'm more concerned about you. Are you sure you don't want to go to the emergency room?"

Claire took a deep breath and said with a shake in her voice, "Brian, I'm okay, but it's more than an accident. Something is going on with me. My vision is blurry. I thought I just scratched a cornea with my contact lens or something, and it's just in the one eye. But now, this numbness. I feel like I can't lift my arms. Something is really wrong with me," Claire said.

"Let's call the doctor then, okay, sweetie?" Brian took his cell phone out of his pocket, looked up Claire's doctor's number on the internet, then made the call. He handed the phone to Claire.

After interrogating her with a series of questions and determining that she wasn't in immediate danger, Dr. Morrison said with concern, "This situation calls for some tests at the hospital, Claire. You need a series of MRIs. I can set that all up for you."

☙

The tests were completed a week later.

When the results were ready, Dr. Morrison called Claire and asked her to come into the office.

"Claire, I wish I had better news. I suspect that you have multiple sclerosis. We did find a lesion on your spine, and the optic nerve in your left eye has been affected, too. I am so sorry to tell you this. Right now, there is nothing more we can do but watch you closely to see if your disease progresses to MS. If it is MS, we do know the disease is chronic and will likely continue to worsen—to what degree we don't know. That is the nature of it. There are treatments, of course, and we will do everything we can to help you," Dr. Morrison gave her a sad but matter-of-fact look. "Right now, I am prescribing steroids so we can resolve your vision. You will likely have all, if not most, of your vision restored. As for your arms, be careful you don't overuse your body. Look into apps and tools you can use in place of typing, for instance. Get a little more help around the house. This is a great excuse to hire a house cleaner." He smiled, clearly trying to cheer her up. She nodded with a small grim smile and Dr. Morrison resumed his professional demeanor.

Claire sighed with sadness. It was like the whole future she had envisioned, first with Alan, and now with Brian, had just been dreams. She could still have her little family, but how what would the rest of her life be like? Would she need a wheelchair? Maybe in twenty or thirty years, she wouldn't even be able to walk. *And what about Danny? How can I care for him when I can't even hold him?*

She was smart enough to know she was in shock. Dr. Morrison rattled on about follow-up appointments, referrals to different specialists, and resources she might want to look into. Claire heard the words whirling past her head, but she couldn't grasp their meanings—or understand how they pertained to her life.

My God, how will I tell Brian?

Brian wasn't a shallow man, and Claire knew his love for her ran deep, but she felt so guilty, condemning him to live with a partner who couldn't keep up. Who might always have to sit on the sidelines as life passed her by. Could she do that to him? Pin him down like that? It was true they weren't married yet, but they had certainly talked about it and started dreaming of their life together. She had to consider him.

Brian was in the waiting room taking care of Danny. He had driven Claire to the appointment, insisting that even if he couldn't go in, he would be as close by as possible. As she walked down the hall, on legs she could barely feel due to the shock of Dr. Morrison's words, she spotted him. He smiled. Claire smiled back automatically, but her heart was a lead weight.

She neared him as her mind went into overdrive. *When should I tell him? When we get in the car? When we get home? Will I be able to tell him without becoming almost hysterical?*

Brian could tell by Claire's expression that the news wasn't good. The smile slid off his face, replaced by concern. There was no denying the alarm in his eyes.

"Sweetheart," he jogged over to her, bouncing Danny in his seat as he did. Claire smiled a little more genuinely at the sight of her two boys and Brian's obvious dedication. "What is it? What did the doctor say?" Two lines appeared in the middle of Brian's forehead, and Claire had to stop herself from reaching out and smoothing them with her finger. Even in the midst of this life-changing shock, she didn't want anything so painful to touch his life. But she was about to share words that she could never take back.

She managed a weak smile and thankfully fought back her tears. "How about we wait until we are back at my apartment?" Claire said, laying her hand on Brian's arm. "Everything is okay. It's nothing fatal, but I need a little more time to digest this and hopefully find some control. I don't want to cry in public."

"Well, I will say I am partially relieved." The lines between Brian's eyes diminished, but when he grabbed her hand, his grip was firm, protective.

The drive back to Claire's apartment was quiet with Claire stealing looks at Brian's face. She loved him, and he was doing a poor job of hiding his worry.

Once inside her apartment, Brian laid Danny down quickly, then returned to the couch to take Claire's hand and stare directly into her eyes.

"I just want you to know that whatever you have to tell me, we can handle it together. I will always be here for you." He squeezed her hand as the first tear since the appointment leaked out of her eye.

Claire took a big breath in and blew it out. She put her other hand on Brian's, and he added his free one to the top, so they were clutching onto each other with all they were worth. "Go ahead," he urged gently, and Claire related everything the doctor had said. As she spoke, Brian's face showed the pain he was feeling. His eyes filled with tears, and soon, they were crying together.

"I hope I will be enough for you still," Claire's voice was a watery whisper. "It feels like someone ran me off the road."

It was true. Life was going so well. They were about to make some wonderful plans. They'd talked about moving to a big house with enough room for Danny to run around. They would care for each other and all live together as an unbreakable trio.

Brian turned her news over and over in his mind. Claire could see the wheels turning. He gently said, "We may have to adjust fire, but we can still do so much of what we talked about. I love you, Claire, and I will always care for you, no matter the circumstances, ALWAYS!"

Brian's response rendered Claire speechless. All she could feel was his adoration and gratitude mixed in with her loss and the consequences. It was such an odd blend of emotions.

She cleared her throat. "I have another appointment with the doctor in a couple of days, and we will discuss our plan of attack." She smiled crookedly. It was the best she could do. "Who knows? Maybe it won't be as horrible as we are imagining?"

"Maybe," Brian said hopefully.

"I keep thinking about Danny. I am already worrying about picking him up. What if I drop him?"

"We'll be very careful, and I think I should come stay here to help you out. We can juggle Danny!" And there it was, the spark, the flare, the fire returned to Brian's eyes. In spite of the heavy news of the day, Claire clapped her hand over her mouth and laughed.

Brian flushed red, "Oh!" Sudden dawning appeared on his face. "I didn't mean that. You have to know … I would never really juggle him …"

But Claire was giggling now, the kind of inappropriate laughter that spills out at a funeral. "I know what you meant," she said. "That's why I'm laughing."

"Before I stuck my foot so far in my mouth I could tickle my tonsils, I was going to say, you can hold Danny sitting down, and we will get you all situated with feeding him, even changing him."

"I am so thankful for you, you silly sweetheart!" Claire leaned in to kiss Brian, but he rushed toward her and squeezed her to his chest. Then they did kiss, and a feeling of security swept over her. *Maybe I will be okay.*

As the days and weeks went by, Claire's symptoms worsened. Her new neurologist, Dr. Packer, a lovely Armenian woman, told her this was normal. "MS is a snowflake disease, meaning everyone is affected in different ways. Your rapid heartbeat and fatigue tell me that you are in the middle of your exacerbation. Your lesion on your spine is fresh. For you to start getting better, you need to start healing, and your body has to form scar tissue to give you back some of your normal function. It doesn't mean you will be back to one hundred percent, but you could get close. Rest when you need to, and don't push yourself. Overtiredness and exertion—not to mention stress—can make your symptoms worse."

On the way home in an Uber—since Claire didn't have the strength to drive—the significance of her situation hit Claire with a force that started a fresh deluge of tears. *I have to hire a full-time nanny. I cannot risk dropping Danny, and Brian can't do it all, not while he's at work. I'm not smiling at Danny or even playing with him as I should. It's not fair to him. He deserves more.* But she wanted to be that more. She wanted to be his mommy in all ways. The next best thing was Margie, and Claire was thrilled to learn that Margie could handle the job and wanted it full time. Danny enjoyed being with Margie, which was the most important part of the decision.

Work seemed to sap a lot of the little bit of energy Claire had, and she was considering quitting. Although the thought of leaving the firm about cracked her heart in half.

With Margie attending to Danny, Claire retreated to her bedroom after her appointment. Brian was at work in client appointments and unable to get away. Sure, Margie had picked up the slack, but Claire missed him. She knew as she lay there that she was feeling sorry for herself. *Better not make this a habit!* she told herself. *No sense in making it worse.*

Brian had already broached the idea of her quitting, so she knew he was on board. But there was something about providing for herself and Danny. It wasn't that she needed to be independent, she wanted to. She wanted the choice of what her life would be. Giving up her job was not a decision she would have made on her own. She could understand mothers staying home and being with their children, and she would have chosen differently if she'd had the choice—to not fully lose herself in one life or another—but live in a combination of both.

Now it was too late. Her path had been set. Without her permission, without her desire. And dwelling on it wasn't going to help—but she wanted to. It was tempting to curl up in a cocoon where it was dark and small and stay there. She could cry and be in denial as long as she wanted to.

Suddenly, she was angry. *I can't even do that!* The anger was her tipping point. She didn't want to become that person. All her life, she'd refused to be so ugly and negative. *I will not let whatever this is get to me. I won't let it change me.*

Claire got up and sat on the edge of the bed. "I'll have to make some major changes," she said, finding there was strength in her voice after all. Sometimes, it was hard to talk about this new chapter in her life. *Fine, I will talk to myself.* She smiled a little at the thought of having a conversation with herself. *Back to basics, kid.* "I have to give up this beautiful apartment for one thing, but maybe I could work part-time. Would Mr. Andrews agree to that?"

A knock at the door startled her. "Claire, are you on the phone? Are we out of baby wipes? I'm sorry I can't seem to find them, and I have a half-naked Danny in his crib."

"I'll be right there!" Claire said, laughing at the thought of Danny ready to do his worst in the crib and poor Margie. She opened the door and walked across the hall to Danny's room, still trying to figure out her predicament. *If I could find an apartment where the rent isn't too high, and I give up ALL spending on personal items, maybe I could make it?* Sure, Brian was all too happy to be the provider, but Claire couldn't depend on that—not yet.

Chapter 19

That evening, after dinner, Claire explained to Brian her thoughts about moving somewhere less expensive and possibly working part-time. As soon as she mentioned the money factor, Brian interrupted, "Sweetheart, I have wanted to talk to you about a wonderful plan I have. I am Alan's only living relative and survivor. He left everything to me. His insurance policy, his stocks, his savings, EVERYTHING. It is a rather sizable amount, and I know without the slightest doubt that he would want me to share it with you. What do you think of the idea of buying a lovely lake house? Maybe in Michigan? The three of us could live very comfortably, and you have to know how very much I want us to be together."

"Oh—kay, that sounds almost too good to be true. What's the first step?"

"Leave the planning to me."

"I mean, I guess I could leave work. At least I would be around Danny full time. But Margie … and are you going to get established somewhere else? What about your patients? It's such a lovely thought, Brian, and maybe it could work out." She paused and chuckled. "Gosh! My mind has been nonstop lately!"

"I can only imagine. And I do know, to a degree. I'm affected differently, but never doubt that we're in this together."

"Brian, I didn't mean to leave you out. I just never want to impose."

"You're going through so much, and you are doing great, my love. It's going to feel awkward talking about this new situation and everything that entails for both of us. That's okay. We'll be gentle with each other. I never think you're shutting me out. Never."

From his smile, Claire could see he was serious.

"Sooooo … I have something else to run past you. It's a bit of a crazy thought, but in many ways, a beautiful one."

"Certainly, I would love to hear what you are thinking," Brian said eagerly.

"It might sound like lunacy at first, but after you give it some serious consideration, you will come to realize it has some merit. At least, that's where my mind is right now."

"Now I am intrigued. Go on," Brian urged.

There was no other way to say it but just to come straight out with it.

"What would you think of us finding Bryce's family? I believe they live on the East Coast. I was thinking of visiting them and asking them to raise Danny. It's just one option I'm considering, the other being what you brought up today. I just feel so helpless, and I don't want Danny to ever know the circumstances of his conception. I don't want him to see his mother as sick and helpless, either."

Brian's face fell, but he nodded, and Claire charged on, not even recognizing her voice as she laid out the steps of the plan.

"I have no idea if they would accept an idea like this. It sounds quite bizarre, I know." Tears welled in her eyes. She was trying to be so strong and talk about this alternative with strength, to do the best for Danny, but she was already failing.

After a long pause, Brian spoke, shock punctuating his every word.

"My God, Claire, you would and moreover *could* give up Danny? I know you love him, and he is your son, too. What a selfless thought. I can't really share my thoughts right now as they are too selfish. And I don't have a stake in this either. I will do whatever you think is best."

"Thank you," she whispered, nearly no volume in her voice.

"You are amazing, Claire, and I love you so very much."

Claire thought she could enlist Ellie or Vida to help locate Bryce's family. The next day back at work, she asked them if they would talk to Mr. Andrews and make some very low-key inquiries about Bryce's family. She needed at least a place to begin searching to find an address.

Ellie went to Mr. Andrew's office and out of the blue, rambled out the story she had rehearsed. "Interesting fact, Mr. Andrews, I have been invited to visit a former school friend living on the East Coast. When she told me the name of the city and neighborhood, it rang a bell. Am I wrong in remembering that Mr. Hollingsworth was from Charlotte, North Carolina?"

"That seems right," Mr. Andrews answered. "Funny what the mind remembers. Let me find his funeral notice." He pulled open a desk drawer and rummaged around. "Here it is!" he exclaimed triumphantly, waving a clipping in the air.

"You are right about the city, and it even lists his neighborhood, Eastover. Do you think your friend lives in the same neighborhood too? Wouldn't that be a small world?"

Ellie grinned. "It sure would! But I doubt that my friend is from there. It sounds like an upscale area to me—my friend isn't that well off. Anyway, thanks so much, Mr. Andrews! I appreciate your open-door policy—even if it is just to ask a silly question."

"No such thing, Ellie," Mr. Andrews said, holding up a finger.

Ellie had no idea why Claire was interested in finding out more about the late bastard Bryce but figured she would share in time.

She went from Mr. Andrew's office to Claire's desk, sing-songing her findings, "Jackpot, babe! Mr. Andrews knew the city and even the neighborhood. Of course, he didn't give me an address, and I didn't ask. Didn't want to look like a stalker!"

Claire obliged her with a chuckle. "Okay, Sherlock, thank you for your help. I bet I can find what I am looking for if I do a little surfing."

Ellie bit the inside of her mouth to keep from asking the question that wanted to burst from her lips: *Why do you care about Bryce Hollingsworth?*

☙

After Scotty's last escape from the hospital, and with a kitchen knife, no less, when he was apprehended again, he was thrown into a maximum security room. The room was small, with a tiny window and metal bars. "Here you go, Houdini," the stout officer said, "I haven't lost anyone yet." Scotty scoffed as he was encouraged to keep moving farther away from the entrance, then the officer dragged the heavy steel door shut and locked it from the outside. A window in the middle was large enough to slide in a meal tray, a few books, and nothing else. Even if he could have fit his hand through, the lock was high enough up on the outside of the door that Scotty couldn't reach it.

Scotty was miserable and vowed to himself that he would find a way out. His nightmares were increasing as the drugs he had been on passed out of his system. Every night when he lay down, the dreams came. The most vivid dreams involved him killing or hurting someone. It wasn't the hurt he inflicted that bugged him. He just wanted to sleep through the night. He'd told the nurse all about it when he was admitted.

The first night in his new cell, after a rude knock on his door, Scotty opened the window to find a Dixie cup full of pills. Next came a small cup of water to wash them down.

"Lift your tongue, Hawkins!" another officer said, this one was shorter and broader. Scotty decided he resembled a pig man. But he did as the man asked, showing his open mouth through the small window. He wasn't curious enough to find out what would happen if he rebelled. *And maybe the pills will let me sleep till morning.*

One night several weeks later, Scotty was lost in more dreams of bloodshed and agonizing cries when he rose up from the layers of sleep to the sound of sirens. His pills had done nothing but dull his senses and make him not care. They hadn't touched his dreams. In a daze, Scotty didn't know if the sharp pealing alarms were real or part of his dreams. As he got his bearings and blinked sleep from his eyes, it was undeniable.

The sirens were real. But what did they mean? Suddenly, he heard one of the orderlies doing something with the lock on his door. "Everybody out," he shouted, hammering on Scotty's door. "Get out, Hawkins! Run! The building is on fire! Go to the quad by the front doors and wait on the lawn. Don't you try to run either!" The man yelled as he moved down the hall to bang on another door and spring another patient free. "We will find you! Stay by the quad. Wait for your section orderly to count you up!" Bang, bang, "Mayer! Rise and shine. Get out here!" And on he went while Scotty stood there, smoke stinging his lungs, his heart pounding.

He slid on a pair of slippers, grabbed the journal from under his pillow, and hurried out the door. Scotty ran down the corridor and took the cement stairs two at a time. Then he was *out* the front door! *Am I really outside? Is this real and not a dream?* He was almost afraid to believe any of it was true.

Soon several fire trucks appeared and, as Scotty skirted the trees in the side yard, concealing himself in the shadows, he knew this was his second chance. This time he would not screw up. This time, he was FREE! And he would stay that way!

"Hawkins," came the lead orderly's voice. It struck his ears like a club upside the head. "Hawkins? Dammit! Get over here! Didn't I say to gather outside? Now, where is Hawkins?"

That was it. Scotty was on the move. The voice commanding his presence and to report back to his cell was just dregs on the wind now. It mixed in with the smoke and got lost in his mind. Scotty didn't care. He wasn't dumb, not like everyone thought anyway. He stuck to the shadows for a long, long time, slipping this way and that through the streets. He made sure never to walk in a straight and predictable line— like he was fleeing an alligator. He'd learned that in a science book when he was a kid. If you were ever being chased by an alligator, best to run in a zigzag. Scotty was being chased in a way. So that's what he did. And no one came for him.

It was just the black shiny tar of the road glistening under the moon and him. He was alone ... for now.

Chapter 20

Claire was obsessing over the plan to contact the Hollingsworths. It would be the hardest letter she would ever have to write, and she tried to do it while staying tethered to Danny. She and Brian had decided that a handwritten letter would be the least intrusive. A phone call might be suspected as a scam, and showing up on their doorstep with the baby seemed grotesque.

To do it, she had to think of herself as not just Danny's mother. She was his protector. That mindset made it a little easier. Still, her hand shook as she positioned the pen over the paper. It was hard to hold onto it. It kept wanting to slip out of her grasp. She still struggled with a lack of strength in her arms, too, but even if it looked like a chicken scratch, Claire would get it done. She just couldn't stop thinking about all the Hollingsworths had to offer her little boy and what had been stolen from her.

After working at it a while, Claire repositioned the pen in her fingers and prepared to write the first word. Her heart broke for the millionth time that year, and Claire swallowed back a lump in her throat as she tried to be logical.

Which way would come off as the most sincere, honest, heartfelt approach?

Then she very carefully and slowly started writing. Writing the words made the situation more real. Now the pen shook as she put down her message.

Dear Mrs. Hollingsworth,

First of all, I would like to introduce myself. My name is Claire Kendall, and I work at the marketing firm in Chicago, where your son Bryce was the CEO.

Bryce and I were intimate just once, and that resulted in my becoming pregnant. I delivered a baby boy, and I thought you should know that you have a healthy, adorable grandson.

If you care to learn more, you may contact me ... My address is on the return of the envelope.

Sincerely,

Claire Kendall

Claire read the letter over and over before she decided to mail it. "Now we wait and see if she responds, and what her response will be." It was hard to hold back her tears and, this time, she didn't stop them. With Danny and Margie in the next room and Brian at work, Claire let every last tear fall from her face until she was dehydrated. She secretly hoped that her idea to have the Hollingsworths raise Danny was a bust. *At least I could say I tried.*

⁂

Scotty ran wildly. Tears streamed down his face. He had no idea where he was going; all he knew was he was OUT! Suddenly it started to rain. Soon, his shirt and slippers were soaking. He knew he had to get some cover and finally found a dumpster with big cardboard boxes inside. He grabbed them and tore them apart, putting one piece on the ground, underneath himself, and another over himself. At least he had some protection. Finally, he fell asleep to the sound of the rain pattering on his makeshift cardboard blanket. Strangely, it was soothing, and he didn't dream of murdering anyone. His sleep was a cloak, blotting out any light until the sun colored the world around him and dried up some of the moisture.

Scotty lifted up his head from his mat and shoved off his cardboard blanket to find an unkempt man with long straggly white hair, almost as long as his white beard, walking by. He poked at Scotty's soggy slipper with a beat-up walking stick and said, "Hey Bro, you new to the neighborhood? What's your name?"

"My name is Scott, not that it's any of your business," hissed Scotty. He retreated under his cardboard blanket and hoped the guy would go away.

"Whoa, hold on there, Scott," the man said, lowering Scotty's "blanket." "I was just going to ask if you would like to walk down the street for a cup of coffee at the soup kitchen. It's pretty damn good, and it's free!"

"Oh, yeah okay. Sounds good. What's your name?" Scotty asked as he pushed his bedding off to the side. The man offered his hand to help him stand up.

"My name is Arthur, but my friends call me Artie. And you must be sore, sleeping like that. Not that I haven't been there, 'cause, boy howdy, have I. Now I grab a bed at the shelter right early in the morning. We can head over there and grab two beds after the soup kitchen."

Scotty shrugged and followed Artie to the soup kitchen, happy to get a hot cup of coffee. Suddenly, he realized he wasn't holding the journal. *Where's the journal?*

He raced around, yelling frantically and shaking Artie's filthy clothes, "Where's my journal? Who took my journal?"

Artie tried to calm Scotty, "Ease up, fella. Your journal was sopping wet, and the rain smeared all the writing. You couldn't read a dang thing. I tossed in the dumpster, Scott. The rain erased all of it."

Scotty's eyes grew huge, and he gritted his teeth so loudly they squeaked. Artie took a step back, holding his hands up.

"Calm down! What the hell was so important?"

Scotty didn't answer him. He was off and running again, storming around the soup kitchen, shouting obscenities and knocking over chairs. Artie wisely gave him a wide berth and went to sit at a far table in the corner.

One of the kitchen workers called the authorities, and the police arrived and hauled Scotty away.

It didn't take long before they identified him and escorted him back to the facility, which was mostly operational after the admin offices had caught fire but not spread to the patients' ward. Scotty kicked and screamed all the way until he was safely inside his room; the heavy metal door slammed shut behind him. The sound of the locks engaging echoing.

Once inside his room with his meds taking effect, he would mellow out.

Maybe this is the best place for me. I know Lucy knows I am here, and I am sure she will come soon and bring me home with her to Kokomo. It was something to hold onto, but in the next minute, he forgot who Lucy even was. All he knew was he was very, very tired. He didn't know why, but his feet hurt, and he had a cut on his hand and had no idea how it had gotten there. Scotty crashed onto his bed and succumbed to his dreams. This time, he wasn't the killer but was being killed by a person with no face—and he couldn't wake up.

☙

Days turned into weeks with no response from Mrs. Hollingsworth. Claire was disappointed and relieved at the same time. She told herself her feelings didn't matter. She had to and would always do what was best for Danny. As the days dragged on, she slowly accepted that her idea would not work out. Then her mind was off on another adventure. *How the hell will I take care of him the way he needs?* She went back to waiting and tried not to think about the result one way or the other.

Two days later, the response did arrive.

> *Dear Ms.? Miss.? Mrs.? Kendall,*
>
> *(I have no idea which it is.)*
>
> *After reading your ridiculous letter, I have come to the conclusion that you are a lying bitch, and are only trying to extort money from me. Bryce never mentioned your name, nor that he had gotten a woman pregnant.*
>
> *It is sad to think how low some people will stoop.*
>
> *You, and your bastard son, can go to hell.*

Mrs. M. Hollingsworth

Claire couldn't believe the anger and outrage she read in Mrs. Hollingsworth's words. Not only did she feel sad that there was no possibility of having Bryce's family adopt and raise Danny, but there was also no chance they would ever want to see him. He would never know that side of his family. Even though she accepted in the deepest recesses of her mind that she was in no way responsible—except for having green teeth!—she couldn't help but feel she had failed her son.

Claire regarded the letter and the thin spiky writing that scolded her from the page. *Their loss*, she thought.

"Brian," Claire called from where she sat at the dining room table to her office, where Brian had moved his practice to. "I finally heard from Mrs. Hollingsworth, and the response was not good." She walked toward the office and gave Brian a half smile. "Here, read it for yourself."

Brian quickly scanned the note, then reached for Claire, and gave her a big hug. "Don't let this nasty letter upset you, sweetheart. We have other options. Options that are probably better in the long run."

"I'm relieved and angry all at once."

"Of course you are," Brian soothed. "I won't tell you how happy I am right now. Just feel how you need to feel." But he had a dopey smile on his face, and Claire realized he not only loved her, but he loved Danny. It hit her then. He had started to think of himself as his father. The realization took away any negative feelings. She would consider what to do about Danny's other side of the family later.

"Brian, I would like to hear what options you are considering. I know you have grown so attached to Danny, and I can't help but think I have hurt you. That you must have felt so powerless. That was never my intention."

"Claire, honey, love has no geography. I will always love Danny and be there for him no matter who has the privilege of raising him."

All Claire could do was hug him. "So you really think everything is going to be okay and that Danny won't lack for anything even though God knows what state I might be in?" Her words muffled in his chest, but she couldn't bring herself to meet his eyes.

"No matter what happens, even if you can't walk, run, skip, hop, or whatever, you will always have your heart. Danny will feel that. Anything else can be figured out. It's just logistics."

Claire did raise her head to peer up into his soulful eyes then. She still couldn't speak around the thickness in her throat and the tears on the brink of falling.

"Sweetheart," Brian kissed her on the top of her head. "I was thinking that we should build that beautiful lake house I've been talking about. We could add on a related living area—or hell, even a separate house—and hire a full-time nanny if Margie doesn't want to relocate."

Claire nodded. She wished she could show Brian her heart. No words sufficed to explain the depth of appreciation and love washing through her.

"I want us to be married, and I want to adopt Danny, to take care of you. Of the both of you. Please say yes to all of my ideas. Please, Claire. It would be my honor to care for my family."

How could one person have so much caring and love inside? Brian was truly an amazing man, and Claire loved him so much. "Yes, yes, and yes, Brian. I love you more than I can ever explain, I am so grateful for you and am the luckiest woman in the world."

Brian heaved a big sigh. "I know it's silly, but I was afraid for a minute that you'd say no!" He issued a shaky little chuckle.

"In time, you and I will both understand my feelings about considering the Hollingsworths. I guess I just panicked. I felt so small and useless like all I can do now is fail him. He deserves so much! I didn't know if I'd gotten it all wrong … like I wasn't supposed to be his mother. This prognosis blew my mind in the worst way, and I don't want to be a burden to anyone, not to you or Danny. I just wanted to run and give you both back your lives. You can make a choice, and I know you want to marry me like I want to marry you. Well, I thought, he's a grown man, he knows what he's doing, choosing me. But Danny … how could I live with myself if I was so selfish? And now, how can I live with myself for even thinking of relinquishing him?"

"I have never met someone so hard on themselves as you." Brian took Claire's hand and led her to the chair in the corner. He eased her down into it and knelt at her knee. "Cut yourself a break. Let yourself feel all the things. Every good and bad feeling. It's all normal. Then, for God's sake, please forgive yourself—for what, I don't know."

"You are one hell of a therapist," Claire said, wiping her tears away with the tips of her fingers.

"I'm going to be an even better husband. Just you watch," Brian said, taking her hands in his. He kissed her full on the lips, and Claire let herself fall into his love, into his soft lips, into the scent of him. She drank him in.

When they pulled apart, Claire said with a new bright note in her voice, "Let's get started with all your wonderful ideas."

"First things first." Brian's face split into the most expansive smile ever. "Our wedding. I want it to be fabulous, beautiful, gorgeous, and just about any other wonderful adjective you would care to add. My darling Claire, you deserve the best wedding, and I plan to see that you shall have exactly that!"

Their talk turned to wedding plans as they sat there in the office, their former cares nearly forgotten.

They decided the wedding would be small with just a few guests. Claire hoped Chloe would agree to be matron of honor, and she planned to ask Ellie and Vida to be bridesmaids. Melissa could be the flower girl, and Michael, the ring bearer. Brian grinned at all her ideas and added his own.

Brian would ask his cousin Al to be the best man. They would arrange to be married in a small chapel. A lovely old restaurant in the country they had eaten at a couple of times and adored would be ideal for the reception.

Claire's thoughts wandered to her wedding gown and the other gals' dresses. She pondered over the flowers and music. As she sat there deep in thought with Brian, she put her illness out of her mind. Distraction was a joyful remedy as she allowed herself to finally feel pure joy.

Claire knew Brian was anxious to become her husband, and she loved him all the more for his impatience. After speaking with the chapel they loved the most, they landed on a date.

In the interim, Claire and Brian decided it would be best for Danny to remain at home with Margie while they wed. She secretly thought that having Danny in the pictures would raise a lot of questions for him later. Of course, Brian planned to adopt Danny, and Danny would know Brian as his daddy in his formative years, but he would be told about the adoption when he was old enough to understand. *It's really going to come in handy that his father's a therapist!*

Suddenly, the wedding was just three weeks away! Claire wondered how all their plans could fall into place in such a short time.

For her wedding dress, Claire chose a white silk gown with billows of extra layers in the back that flowed when she walked. It was sleeveless and form-fitting, which showed off her slender figure.

Chloe, Ellie, and Vida wore a similar style in blush pink.

The day arrived, and everything turned out just as everyone had hoped. Claire felt fairly well, and her happiness showed on her radiant face.

When Claire saw Brian standing at the altar, so handsome in his gray tuxedo, a tear fell down her cheek. She determined to stop crying in case she ruined her makeup. That would never do for the photos they would be looking back at for years to come.

The wedding was beautiful. Melissa and Michael did a fantastic job, and

Claire was so proud of her niece and nephew. They seemed to understand the importance of the day and kept glancing up at her as they walked evenly down the aisle, as if to say, *am I doing this right?* She nodded and gave them encouraging smiles, which they returned on their impish faces.

At the reception, everyone wished the happy couple much happiness, and each person silently prayed Claire and Brian would have many years together. Claire's illness hung like a dark cloud in everyone's mind but it never came up in conversation, and she was grateful to have a different focus, at least for one day.

When the last of the guests had trickled out into the night, Brian turned to Claire with a mischievous expression.

"Now, my beautiful bride, after I show you how very much I love you, I hope maybe tomorrow we can start planning our lovely home together," he said.

"Yes, my handsome husband, I am anxious to get started on our plans, too. *Despite our little curveball, life is good, Claire thought. It's not perfect, but no one's life is.*

Claire and Brian enjoyed a small honeymoon for a few days, staying at one of the most expensive hotels in Chicago and dining at all the best restaurants. They called home and checked on Danny frequently, relieved to learn that he had not completed a milestone without them.

As expected, as soon as they returned home, Brian called his favorite architect to start planning their new home on the lake.

Brian had such a new sense of purpose in everything he did. He told Claire frequently how his life had more meaning and that he felt so positive about their future. At every chance he got, he reassured her how he was determined to make each and every one of her coming days as healthy and happy as he possibly could.

"I am such a damn lucky guy," he said to her. "How could someone as wonderful, gorgeous, and smart, etcetera, etcetera, etcetera, ever fall for a guy like me?"

"Are you talking to yourself again, silly? For once and for all, I told you, I am the lucky one!"

Brian was looking for a suitable lot for their house when he came across a beautiful house in a perfect location. Yes, it needed some work, but the front porch faced the lake, and the rooms were just what he had in mind. A lovely kitchen overlooked a beautiful garden, and there were three bedrooms, the primary bedroom, and a large en suite bathroom on the main floor. Two bedrooms on the second floor and another bathroom. PERFECT!!!

It wasn't the house he'd started planning, but it was going to be better. They could add a separate cottage for someone to live with them full time and help take care of Danny. He couldn't wait to show the house to Claire.

Of course, Claire was thrilled with the house and all of Brian's considerations. He always anticipated anything she might need in the future. They made plans to buy the house and move in as soon as possible.

Claire and Brian weren't the only ones making changes in their lives. Ellie announced over lunch with Claire and Vida one day that she and Joe were moving to Arizona, where Joe's job was taking him. That left Vida as the last of the three friends still working at the firm. Just three short works earlier, to the chagrin of Mr. Andrews, Claire had resigned.

On the night that Ellie shared her news, Claire told Brian over dinner, "I have an idea …"

The next day, Claire and Brian approached Vida and asked if she would be interested in moving to the lake. "Of course, you'll have your own place. But your main job would be helping to care for Danny."

Vida, who, as long as Claire had known her, had always had a together exterior, melted on the spot. She was thrilled to be a part of their lives and lend a hand in raising the "little prince," as she called him.

After a short time, the new little family was all settled into their home on the lake. Vida was ecstatic to have her own place right next door and started decorating it right away.

Things were working out well, and everyone was very happy with the arrangement, including Danny.

Claire appreciated her newfound stability, her compassionate husband, her perfect little boy, and her closest friend right next door. She forgot once more about living in fear of the other shoe dropping.

Chapter 21

Several years had passed with Vida loving the arrangement of caring for Danny. Her romantic life hadn't worked out—but not for lack of trying. Claire reassured her she was just such a free spirit; she wasn't meant to be tied down to anyone or anything. She didn't miss her job at the marketing firm—it had never been a great fit for her, although she loved the company—and all three besties had stayed in touch over the years. Ellie was busy with her own family—triplet girls! Joe had opened a dental practice, and she often helped out at his office.

Vida turned to the deep longing in her soul that she'd never given proper time to—art. Ever since she'd been a little girl, she'd had such a talent. Her grandmother had always wanted her to be an art teacher. Vida considered it. After all, Danny was growing up. She wasn't needed as much, and he treated her like a dear aunt who just happened to live on the family compound. Vida had since added a studio in the form of a prefab shed that Brian had mostly built, and she spent many hours in this "she shed," creating whatever spoke to her. Claire loved her paintings. She and Brian bought several of them, framed them, and hung them in the house.

She encouraged Vida to keep painting even while listening to Vida's lamentations that "Life has passed me by. What? Am I really supposed to try and resuscitate some sort of career?"

"Yes!" Claire and Brian both answered together before breaking into giggles of the sort that only belong to a couple who is joined in their thoughts. Vida startled as if like someone had poked her. She chuckled and cut into her steak. They were all sitting on the deck overlooking the water. It was late summer and hot for the time of day. Everyone had the look of people who lived on the water. The tousled hair, burnished skin, and lean, muscled bodies. That was the day Vida had gone all in. She remembered reading somewhere that one day will be the last day you ever need to supervise your child, but you won't know it. And while Danny wasn't hers exactly, they all shared him. Her time for caring for him had come to a close.

The next day, Vida signed up for watercolor lessons, and in a short period, she became quite good. Living in a small town provided just the setting she needed to display her paintings at yearly art fairs.

With Danny becoming more independent, Vida's life changed dramatically—it became hers again. But she and Danny had a bond that would never break.

Claire and Brian told Vida they hoped she would stay on in her house as long as she wanted.

"I hope you never leave," Claire told her one day, taking her hand. "You've become another sister to me. But if you do want to go and spread your wings, I will understand and learn to love you from afar."

Shortly after that talk, with excitement in her amber eyes, Vida ran up to Claire one day and thrust the newspaper at her. "Massive Area Art Show Needs Artists for July 22nd Exhibits."

"Oh Vida! It's like they printed this just for you! You've got to go for it. You've made so much progress since you took that first class. Please say you'll do it!" Claire's whole face lit up as she pleaded with her friend, who was dancing from one foot to the other.

"I'm so afraid to do this!" Vida exclaimed, clapping her hands together and adding a little hop to her back-and-forth dance. "That's how I know I have to do this! Millennium Park, here I come!"

"Yes!" Claire clasped her hands together and raised them over her head like a prizefighter. Vida rolled her eyes and laughed, then gave Claire a quick squeeze and ran off squealing to her studio.

Vida had one month to prepare for the show in downtown Chicago. She would return to her roots—the old stomping grounds of her twenties.

She twirled around her studio, taking stock of the pieces there, and mentally tabulating the other paintings she would need to create. Her mind was always alive with so many ideas she couldn't keep up. The only thing she had to worry about was speed. There was no time to waste. A tiny little voice in the back of her head tried to argue that it was too soon; she'd only just started her artist career. She gleefully told the voice to *shut the hell up!*

She skimmed the article again, reading about the fee and how to enter, that the park would supply the tables and secure the artists' spots. It was time to get to work!

Vida worked at finishing her signature piece and several smaller ones all day long. Her artwork was progressing nicely. Claire was her biggest fan.

Finally, the big day arrived, but Vida would be on her own. Claire and Brian had no choice but to take Danny to Purdue in Lafayette, Indiana. He'd nabbed one of the coveted appointments to meet with an academic director, and they couldn't reschedule. Vida was disappointed, but she understood and was thrilled for Danny. Without the rest of her family, Vida would launch solo. It was almost appropriate to take this next step herself. She would have to get used to breaking away from raising Danny.

The show was a huge success, and Vida sold nine paintings. She was getting attention, and the organization that put on the exhibit had made an appointment to speak with her about more opportunities to share her work. After collecting her money and ensuring the sold paintings were wrapped properly for their new owners, Vida just had to schlep five paintings back to her van. Then she could head home and decide what to do with her newfound funds and connections.

As she loaded the paintings into the van, she suddenly felt a sharp pain in her neck. At first, she thought she'd hit herself on something, but there was no thought after that. The pain was blinding, and she slumped to the ground.

A shadow fell over her, and Vida heard an all-too-familiar voice—belonging to that man-boy. "So, little miss liar, how does it feel to have payback?" Scotty's grinning face leered at her. Vida clasped her hand to her neck and fought to stay awake. "You shouldn't have lied to me about the compact. I could have blackmailed Claire and married Lucy. You ruined everything, and now I ruin you."

Scotty stared at Vida's crumpled body lying on the dirty asphalt parking lot. He gripped the knife he'd stolen from the hospital, that he'd escaped again. Blood dripped from the blade and stained the pavement. As he stood there, nearly breathless at his victory, he moved past Vida and the paintings strewn around her. Then he started slashing the paintings, screaming, "No loss here! You should have stuck to marketing! These paintings are crap, crap, crap! No wonder they didn't sell. You are such a loser, Vida!"

Then he took off running, and the last sound Vida heard was his laughter growing fainter and fainter.

Vida lost consciousness. A passerby found her on the street. Scotty didn't go far. There were too many witnesses. People sprang into action, trying to save her as the blood poured out of her neck. A few beefy-looking men had a squirming Scotty up against the wall, and he couldn't break free no matter how much he fought back. When the police arrived, they hauled him off to jail.

Vida was rushed to the hospital, but she died later that day—before Claire had any idea that Scotty had gotten loose and stabbed her dearest friend.

∽

As the months rolled by, Claire's illness progressed, and her symptoms worsened. Her memory failed her more often, and her gait became unsteady, even with a walker. Her thoughts often drifted to Vida and how she hadn't been with her closest friend on the day she died. It was another instance of not being responsible but feeling all the weight of her involvement. It didn't help her physical state, but Claire presumed it sped up the progress of what was inevitable.

Soon Claire was confined to a wheelchair, which broke her heart, but at least she could still get outside to the lake. Brian had thought of everything and had a ramp installed that ran right to the water. He also put another ramp in the garage to get Claire into the car. They used it not only for her doctor appointments but for leisurely drives. Sometimes Brian would drive Claire into town just so she could see the store windows or stop for an ice cream. She loved window shopping with him and the fact that he found excuses to go on dates with her. For her part, Claire did her best to shove away her sadness. Brian deserved the best of her.

Years passed. Danny grew and matured, his sweet disposition ever-present. Claire never worried that he had inherited any of his birth father's genes. By some miracle, he was just like Brian.

Once in a while, Claire would think back to all the things that had happened over the years. She would recall Alan's accident and the pain she'd endured in losing him. That memory still hurt, but the way she thought of Alan had changed. He was sent to her to bring her Brian. Alan had been a guardian of love. Claire supposed this was still true as she just knew he was watching over them all. She could even hear his voice sometimes and was thankful that, unlike other people who had lost loved loves, it remained as faint echoes in her head: *See, Claire, I told you everything would be okay.*

Of course, the rape popped up in her mind, too. It was a life-changing event that had given her Danny, so while she wasn't thankful for it, she did have gratitude for the way it turned out. Still, she always wondered, *what if I had reported the rape? Would I have been held responsible for Bryce's death? Would it have been considered involuntary manslaughter?* All these years later, she could see that worrying about people putting the pieces together, and figuring out that she had pushed Bryce to his death, was a response to the severe physical and emotional trauma she'd endured.

Now, with the sands of time piling up on the bottom of the hourglass of her life, she could finally blow out that collective inhale that had kept her confined for so long. She could freely love her two special guys. She could look forward to more blessings in the future instead of waiting for disaster to strike. Through Brian's support and love and Danny's unconditional adoration, she had finally healed.

The water was calm from where she observed it. It was quiet as a slight breeze whisked her hair back, allowing Claire moments of contemplation.

My best decision was marrying Brian. He has been so caring, patient, and loving. How many men would marry someone so ill? It was confirmed every day that God broke the mold when He made Brian. Danny wasn't far behind in that category.

Just that morning, Claire had caught herself staring at his maturing face. His jaw was getting more angular, and a slight shadow appeared on his upper lip that he complained about shaving. His athletic abilities and academic skills were amazing. Both Claire and Brian were incredibly proud of their son.

Despite all of their good days, their life wasn't perfect. *But whose is*, Claire reasoned as she reveled in the beauty of the lake. The sun kissed her shoulders and warmed her face.

As the years went on, Claire and Brian counted their blessings and were grateful for the many wonderful years they had together.

Consequences be damned!!!!

Acknowledgments

I want to thank my two daughters, Cathy and Wendy, for always encouraging me to "keep going." If they ever became tired of my "pitching" an idea for the book to them, they never showed it. I appreciate and love them dearly.

Thank you to my many friends for always inquiring how the book was progressing and professing such interest. Your support is much appreciated.

About the Author

Shirley Guendling is a lifelong lover of books. Growing up during the Depression in Chicago, Illinois, books were not that plentiful. Money for books? Unheard of.

When there were no new books, Shirley dreamed up stories for the paper dolls she played with.

She and her parents moved to the suburbs when she was in her late teens. There, she met her late husband, Donald.

Shirley and Don had two beautiful daughters, Cathy and Wendy, who gave them four wonderful grandchildren, Jenny, Christine, Brian, and Janet. Her family expanded once more to include four great-grandchildren, Madison, Jackson, Dean, and Emma—all treasures for Shirley.

As the grandchildren grew, Shirley encouraged them to be readers and lovers of books.

When they reached adulthood, Shirley found she needed another outlet to fill her days. That's when the perfect job appeared! Working at the local library! All the old and new books surrounding her were ideal.

For 22 happy years, Shirley worked at the library.

Writing *Consequences* has been a joy. She finds such pleasure when writing. The characters become real, and she cares about them.

She hopes you will feel the same and love *Consequences*—her second book. The first, *I Believed You*, is a murder triangle romp. Both books are available on Amazon.

Made in the USA
Middletown, DE
14 November 2022